Wolf's Surrender: Part of the Immortal Ops World

(Shadow Agents / PSI-Ops)

by

Mandy M. Roth

Wolf's Surrender: Part of the Immortal Ops World
(Shadow Agents / PSI-Ops)
© Copyright 2016, Mandy M. Roth
First Electronic Printing June 2016, Raven Happy Hour LLC
Trade Paperback Printing June 2016
ALL RIGHTS RESERVED.

All books are copyrighted to the author and may not be resold or given away without written permission from the author, Mandy M. Roth.

This novel is a work of fiction and intended for mature audiences only. Any and all characters, names, events, places and incidents are used under the umbrella of fiction and are of the author's imagination and should not be confused with fact. Any resemblance to persons, living or dead, or events or places or locales is merely coincidence.

Published by Raven Happy Hour LLC
Oxford, MS USA
Raven Happy Hour LLC and all affiliate sites and projects are © Copyrighted 2004-2016

Suggested reading order of books released to date

in the

Immortal Ops Series world

Immortal Ops
Critical Intelligence
Radar Deception
Strategic Vulnerability
Tactical Magik
Act of Mercy
Administrative Control
Act of Surrender
Broken Communication
Separation Zone
Act of Submission
Act of Command
Wolf's Surrender
More to come (check www.mandyroth.com for new releases)

Mandy M. Roth Featured Books

Immortal Ops Series

Immortal Ops
Critical Intelligence
Radar Deception
Strategic Vulnerability
Tactical Magik
Administrative Control
Separation Zone
And more (see Mandy's website)

PSI-Ops Series (Part of the Immortal Ops World)

Act of Mercy
Act of Surrender
Act of Submission
Act of Command
And more (see Mandy's website)

Shadow Agents Series (Part of the Immortal Ops World)

Wolf's Surrender
A Dragon Shifter's Duty
And more (see Mandy's website)

Immortal Outcasts (Part of the Immortal Ops World)

Broken Communication
Damage Report
Wrecked Intel
And more (see Mandy's website)

Crimson Ops Series (Part of the Immortal Ops World) Coming Soon!

Wolf's Surrender: Part of the Immortal Ops World (Shadow Agents / PSI-Ops)

Book One in the Shadow Agents Series

Total surrender doesn't come easy to a natural-born alpha. Shape-shifting Special Operative Brad Durant has been held against his will by the enemy for nearly a year. He's given up hope and is fast giving up his will to survive—that is, until a hot-tempered, redheaded succubus is placed in the cell next to his. She calls to his wolf on a primitive level and he won't let anyone or anything harm her. Giving his body to the little minx is easy, but guarding his heart is much harder.

Dedication

To every reader who has fallen in love with the Immortal Ops World as much as I have over the past thirteen years. Thank you!

Praise for Mandy M. Roth's Immortal Ops World

Silver Star Award—*I feel Immortal Ops deserves a Silver Star Award as this book was so flawlessly written with elements of intrigue, suspense and some scorching hot scenes* —Aggie Tsirikas—Just Erotic Romance Reviews

5 Stars—*Immortal Ops is a fascinating short story. The characters just seem to jump out at you. Ms. Roth wrote the main and secondary characters with such depth of emotions and heartfelt compassion I found myself really caring for them* —Susan Holly—Just Erotic Romance Reviews

Immortal Ops packs the action of a Hollywood thriller with the smoldering heat that readers can expect from Ms. Roth. Put it on your hot list…and keep it there! —The Road to Romance

5 Stars—*Her characters are so realistic, I find myself wondering about the fine line between fact and fiction…This was one captivating tale that I did not want to end. Just the right touch of humor endeared these characters to me even*

more — eCataRomance Reviews

5 Steamy Cups of Coffee — *Combining the world of secret government operations with mythical creatures as if they were an everyday thing, she (Ms. Roth) then has the audacity to make you actually believe it and wonder if there could be some truth to it. I know I did. Nora Roberts once told me that there are some people who are good writers and some who are good storytellers, but the best is a combination of both and I believe Ms. Roth is just that. Mandy Roth never fails to surpass herself* — coffeetimeromance

Mandy Roth kicks ass in this story — inthelibraryreview

Immortal Ops Series and PSI-Ops Series Helper
(This will be updated in each upcoming book as new characters are introduced.)

Immortal Ops (I-Ops) Team Members

Lukian Vlakhusha: Alpha-Dog-One. Team captain, werewolf, King of the Lycans, mated to Peren Matthews (Daughter of Dr. Lakeland Matthews). Book: Immortal Ops (Immortal Ops)

Geoffroi (Roi) Majors: Alpha-Dog-Two. Second-in-command, werewolf, blood-bound brother to Lukian, mated to Melissa "Missy" Carter-Majors. Book: Critical Intelligence (Immortal Ops)

Doctor Thaddeus Green: Bravo-Dog-One. Scientist, tech guru, werepanther, mated to Melanie Daly-Green (sister of Eadan Green). Book: Radar Deception (Immortal Ops)

Jonathon (Jon) Reynell: Bravo-Dog-Two. Sniper, weretiger, mated to Tori Manzo. Book: Separation Zone (Immortal Ops)

Wilson Rousseau: Bravo-Dog-Three. Resident smart-ass, wererat, mated to Kimberly (Daughter of Culann of the Council) Book: Strategic Vulnerability (Immortal Ops)

Eadan Daly: Alpha-Dog-Three. PSI-Op and handler on loan to the I-Ops to round out the team, Fae, mated to Inara Nash. Brother of Melanie Daly-Green. Book: Tactical Magik (Immortal Ops)

Colonel Asher Brooks: Chief of Operations and point person for the Immortal Ops Team. Mated to Jinx, magik, succubus, well-known, well-connected madam to the underground paranormal community. Book: Administrative Control (Immortal Ops)

Paranormal Security and Intelligence (PSI) Operatives

General Jack C. Newman: Director of Operations for PSI North American Division, werelion. Adoptive father of Missy Carter-Majors.

Duke Marlow: PSI-Operative, werewolf. Mated to Mercy. Book: Act of Mercy (PSI-Ops)

Doctor James (Jimmy) Hagen: PSI-Operative, werewolf. Took a ten-year hiatus from PSI. Mated to Laney. Book: Act of Surrender (PSI-Ops)

Striker (Dougal) McCracken: PSI-Operative,

werewolf.

Miles (Boomer) Walsh: PSI-Operative, werepanther. Mated to Haven. Book: Act of Submission (PSI-Ops).

Captain Corbin Jones: Operations coordinator and captain for PSI-Ops Team Five, werelion. Mated to Mae Bertelot. Book: Act of Command (PSI-Ops)

Malik (Tut) Nasser: PSI-Operative, (PSI-Ops).

Colonel Ulric Lovett: Director of Operations, PSI-London Division.

Immortal Outcasts

Casey Black: I-Ops test subject, werewolf, mated to Harmony. Book: Broken Communication.

Weston Carol: I-Ops test subject, werebear, mated to Paisley. Book: Damage Report.

Bane Antonov: I-Ops test subject, weregorilla.

Shadow Agents

Bradley Durant: PSI-Ops: Shadow Agent Division, werewolf. Book: Wolf's Surrender.

Ezra: PSI-Ops: Shadow Agent Division, dragonshfiter.

Caesar: PSI-Ops: Shadow Agent Division, werewolf.

Miscellaneous

Culann of the Council: Father to Kimberly (who is mated to Wilson). Badass Fae.

Pierre Molyneux: Master vampire bent on creating a race of super soldiers. Hides behind being a famous art dealer in order to launder money.

Gisbert Krauss: Mad scientist who wants to create a master race of supernaturals.

Walter Helmuth: Head of Seattle's paranormal underground. In league with Molyneux and Krauss.

Dr. Lakeland Matthews: Scientist, vital role in the creation of a successful Immortal Ops Team. Father to Peren Matthews.

Dr. Bertrand: Mad scientist with Donavon Dynamics Corporation (The Corporation).

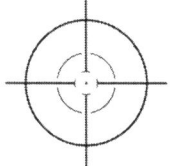

Chapter One

Prologue: Rainforest, South America

Brad Durant ignored the rivulets of sweat dripping down his spine. The wetness pooled at the top of his ass, which wasn't exactly a pleasant feeling. The humidity combined with the temperature had left most of his body covered in a sheen of perspiration. He was used to pushing hard, being soaked and exhausted. This was actually a welcome relief from the last time he'd been in the rainforests of South America, cutting his way through the dense vines of the jungle on a hunt for the enemy—whoever his government had deemed the bad guys at the time. That always changed on a dime.

Now he was just hot.

Well, hot and bored.

Bored out of his mind to be exact.

He'd always excelled at sciences and had truly thought his life's calling might lie with the study of one, but there was no denying his nature. Underneath it all, he was an animal. He needed more to do than study plant samples or discover and classify new species of animals. While that cause was noble, it didn't check all his boxes. He craved action and excitement. His animal needed the hunt—more than what he'd been getting since he'd dived headfirst into higher education. At least the move had been paid for by the government. Seemed the least they could do since he'd devoted so much of his life to them already.

Ironically enough, he'd walked away from a career that held all the danger and excitement he could ever need and more, thinking he wanted to settle down and start a family or something.

A family?

He nearly laughed at the idea of it all now. It wasn't as if something like him—a freak of fucking nature—should have kids. Not without the risk that others would find out what he was or that he'd pass it onto his children. He didn't even want to think on how he'd explain it to the mother if the kids suddenly turned into wolf pups. Funny enough though, when he had dared to let his mind wander on the subject, he would often picture a dark-haired boy holding the hand of a redheaded little girl—the two clearly siblings and both his. But the idea was foolish, and then there was the whole thing about not even knowing if he could have children. If reproduction was even possible.

It wasn't like he'd gotten a handbook when he was in his teens and underwent his first full shift from a human into a wolf. No one magically showed up to walk him through the steps and stages. There was no mentor. No big brother there to lend a guiding hand. There had been fear, pain, more fear, and then shock and awe.

Nothing else. If he did ever find himself lucky enough to discover a woman who loved him even with his defects, and if they managed to be blessed with little ones, he'd be there for the kids every step of the way. Sure, he'd hope they didn't get his abilities, but if they did, he'd help guide them. He'd walk them through a full shift. They'd never be alone like he'd been. They'd never be scared as he was once.

The first time he went through a full shift during the first full moon that occurred during puberty, he'd thought he was dying. That he was being ripped apart from the inside out. It had felt as if every bone in his body had snapped, and he'd believed his skin was going to tear clean off him during it all. The horror of it had made matters worse. Not that the ordeal needed any help. His shifts had gotten easier with age, but his first had been brutal—more so because of his fear and the fact he'd tried to fight it with all he had.

He hadn't understood what was going on. He'd been fine one minute and the next he'd fallen to his knees as his bones felt as if they were breaking one by one, his body contorting, his skin shifting. It had seemed like hours, but looking back it had only taken minutes. And when he'd found himself stuck in the form of an animal, terror had gripped him. He hadn't known if it was permanent and if he was a monster.

If it hadn't been for Vic, Brad would have felt completely and utterly alone in the world. Like a monster spawned forth from the great unknown. Something that should have been hunted and put down. Thankfully, like had attracted like and his best friend had undergone the same changes. The same pain. The same fear. The same worry that they were the only ones.

Mandy M. Roth

Until recently, they'd still believed that to be true. They'd managed to go all through school, join the military, serve their country as Navy SEALs and then work on getting degrees, all while thinking they were freaks — totally alone in the world. And all while doing unthinkable things to hide their secrets from others, from humans. But they weren't the only ones.

There were others out there.

Other men and women who could change forms and shift into animals. Stuff he didn't think could possibly be real was — like vampires and magiks and so much more. He'd learned the truth of it a short time ago and still couldn't stop thinking about it. Learning they each weren't alone was a game changer for both Brad and Vic.

Now, the quest to find a boring career and hide away was no more. The crippling doubt both men had lived with was gone, replaced with hope. They could be part of something finally. Have a family of sorts even — something neither had known in their lives. And soon enough Brad would be back to doing what he'd been trained to do. He'd be back in the field, back doing what he was good at and he'd be done trying to be something he wasn't.

A quiet egghead.

Sighing, he glanced at Vic and lifted a brow as the guide rambled on about the animals who were supposedly known to roam the rainforest area. When the guide got to lions, Brad had to bite his tongue to keep from commenting. The guide was full of shit and seemed to enjoy trying to get one over on his unsuspecting group of tourists.

Vic had suggested they eat the guide twice already. Neither would. The guide smelled like he'd given up bathing some time ago. Not to mention Brad and his friend didn't make a habit of eating humans. Though, there had been an incident while they were in the Middle East that they tended not to bring up much anymore. The guy over there was a sick bastard who had tortured and killed young girls for sport. Vic had lost his shit, shifted forms and made a midnight snack of the asshole.

Jerk had it coming.

"Be careful or the lions will wake and come and kill us all," the guide said, pulling Brad from his thoughts once more. He groaned, and Vic laughed. Unless there were shapeshifters in the area, the tourists were safe from any roaming lions while in the rainforest.

"We better be on guard," joked Vic. "Wait until he finds out there really are wolves here now."

That brought a chuckle from Brad. They'd been tempted to shift forms late at night and run through the jungle to blow off steam, but had been worried they might scare the rest of their tour group should they be spotted. For sure they'd make the guide wet himself. That was nearly enough to make them do it.

The guide in question started in on polar bears being near and Brad couldn't take it anymore. The few people in the group who were still paying attention to the long-winded man actually snorted and made snide comments. The guide tried his best to convince them the polar bear sightings were legit, but it was then he lost what little remaining credibility he'd had with the group.

Vic did a rather fake cough while saying the word "bullshit" and then nudged Brad, motioning in the direction of their fellow classmate, Kim. She'd been one of a large part of the group who had stopped listening to the guide's long talks within the first two days of their arrival. She was currently swatting at another mosquito as she stared miserably around at the wilderness surrounding them. It was plain to see she was not at one with nature, despite her college major being one that would leave her studying plants for life. He snickered as she silently cursed another bug under her breath. He could see a sterile laboratory in her future.

"I'm starting to think she smears honey on herself," said Brad with a lopsided grin. "How else do you explain how much the bugs like her?"

"Mmm, smearing honey on her," Vic murmured, looking far away in thought as he faced Kim.

"Dude, hang it up. In the year we've known her, she has never once looked at you like you stood a chance in the romance department. I'm pretty sure you got friend-zoned within week one."

Vic flashed a wide smile. "Doesn't mean I can't daydream."

"Horndog."

"Asshole."

Brad grinned. "Thanks."

Vic kept staring in Kim's direction. "I feel bad for her. She's covered in bites. At least she listened to you about tucking her pants into her sock tops today. She looked like she had chicken pox yesterday, she was so bit up all over her legs from wearing shorts."

"I'm *sure* your concern for her has a little something to do with her being a hot, black-haired beauty."

Vic grinned. "Maybe. Maybe not."

"Right." Brad snorted. Vic had a type and Kim was it. Tall, leggy and brunette. "Go back to daydreaming about her covered in honey. Like that will ever happen."

Vic shrugged. "Hey, if there was a stacked redhead down here with us, you'd be thinking the same things."

"Damn straight," added Brad with a grin. He had a type too. Hot redheads with big boobs were it. He didn't care how bad it was to admit, he liked a certain type of woman and wasn't ashamed of the fact. His cock twitched at the idea of a sexy little redheaded number making her way to their corner of the rainforest.

Damn.

It had been too long since he'd last had sex. When they got back stateside, he'd head to a bar, hook up with a hottie, didn't matter the color of her hair, and he'd find release. Vic would need to do the same. They'd learned long ago to never push too long without sex. Controlling their animal sides became harder the more time they put between sexual escapades. And neither wanted to come to after a long shift to find out they accidentally ate someone who didn't deserve it.

He grimaced at the idea.

Glancing around, Brad took a deep breath, drawing in the scents of what was near them. He tensed as new smells assaulted him. Their group wasn't large and was filled mostly with other classmates from the university. The few guides they had were now familiar to his senses, and there was, of course, Professor Krauss, who had put together the trip to Brazil to start with. Whatever Brad had gotten a whiff of was not what he'd grown accustomed to on their trip. It was different and not in a good way. It set his wolf on edge, making it want to uncoil from a deep sleep within him. He had to tamp it down for fear of shifting for all to see.

"Everything okay?" asked Vic.

Brad stilled and took in another deep breath, the smell all but gone, and then glanced to his friend. "Yeah. Thought I caught the scent of something, but it was nothing. Guess the heat is getting to me more than I thought."

He could have sworn he sensed a threat near them. It wasn't like him to have false feelings of danger.

"Smelling the lions and polar bears?" Chuckling, Vic stepped closer to him.

Brad laughed. "And then some."

The guide got the show on the road again. Their stops for rest and water were getting longer and longer as of late. Brad and Vic took the lead once more as they were the strongest men in the group and could slice through the thick vines with relative ease compared to the others. Plus, the added exercise went a long way into wearing their animals out.

Kim moved in close behind Vic and Brad knew his buddy was pleased. He also knew Vic wouldn't really make a play for Kim. She'd managed to become something of a friend to them both, and that was rare. They didn't let many people in for fear of their secret being discovered, but there was something about Kim that made them both feel slightly protective of her. Neither guy would dream of screwing that up, not when they had so few friends as it was.

Brad wasn't sure how much time had passed before they came to a clearing and were able to stop cutting vines and branches. It felt as if the jungle was going to close up behind them, instantly regrowing everything they'd just cleared. He looked towards Vic and found him sipping from his canteen and then offering a drink to Kim, who declined. She was still swatting at insects landing on her.

Poor girl. She'd be eaten alive soon.

"Ten-minute break," called the guide.

Vic approached. "Bet this stretches into thirty minutes of his tall tales."

"For sure," offered Brad as he sipped from his own canteen.

"Seems like we were only just here. Hard to believe it's been a few years now, isn't it?"

Brad stiffened at the thought of their active-duty time. There had been a certain thrill to it all—a level of excitement his current area of study lacked in a big way. "Do you miss it?"

Vic glanced away and nodded.

Brad tensed. "What do you think PSI will be like?"

Vic looked around as if worried someone would overhear. Brad wasn't too concerned. It wasn't like anyone with them would even know what PSI stood for. Paranormal Security and Intelligence was a government agency he'd only just learned existed. Humans certainly weren't privy to its presence. Brad was still having a hard time wrapping his head around a clandestine organization consisting of all supernaturals being real, and he was a friggin' shifter.

He and Vic had been approached two months before heading to South America by a recruiter for PSI named Vepkhia. Neither of them had been able to believe a supernatural military agency was real. They'd spent so long hiding in plain sight that they'd been blindsided by the truth of it all. Vepkhia had explained PSI in detail and talked them through everything they needed to know to be brought into the fold. They were excited.

There were many more men and women like them. They were not alone, and it turned out there was a whole policing force dedicated to nothing but the supernatural. It was still surreal. So was the fact that both Brad and Vic had agreed to sign on with PSI. Vepkhia had explained that they'd enter as scientists, able to function as operatives as well. It would be different from their past as SEALs. From what they'd been told they'd be policing supernaturals both locally and abroad. It would be nice to be around others like them and to not have to hide who and what they were.

A refreshing change of pace.

Plus, PSI had been sold to them as being something of a family. A group of men like them. It would be nice to really, truly belong to something and not just pretend. Vic was like a brother to him. They'd grown up together, forming a friendship early on, first out of necessity and then out of loyalty. They'd not been like other children in the foster-care system. And both seemed to have an inborn knowledge that they had to hide the changes they'd started experiencing around the same age they'd first met. A kid didn't need to be brilliant to know that suddenly being able to change into an animal wasn't something one should let others find out about.

Brad still wasn't sure how he'd gotten so lucky as to cross paths with Vic back then, but he had. They'd stayed close, helped one another through the transitioning period and clawed their way out of poverty together. They'd graduated early and joined up with the military, hoping to find a place they'd fit in—where their alpha urges to protect and kill if need be would be useful, not a liability. They'd gone through boot camp and then later BUD/S training together. And now here they were, working on getting their degrees in a field no one would have ever guessed they'd have an interest in—pharmacognosy. He didn't exactly look like the type of guy who wanted to study plants or other natural sources in order to create effective medicines, but he was. That was how they'd ended up in South America, yet again, but this time working under the direction of a brilliant but moody professor.

Professor Krauss had been relatively mild-mannered back at the University, but on this trip he'd been irritable and at times belligerent to Brad and Vic. Neither paid the short, fat man much mind when he started to rant or rave. They could both take him with ease, not that they'd have much of a reason to beat up an old guy. The man was brilliant in his various fields of study, so they overlooked some of his eccentric behavior.

"Break is over," yelled the guide.

Vic groaned as the guide headed down a section of the jungle that he'd sworn earlier was going to be fairly clear. From the heavy amount of vines and overgrowth, the guide was either lost or didn't understand the meaning of clear.

Either way, they'd be cutting their way through the brush once more. Brad stepped forward, ready to do what was needed. Vic moved up and stood beside him.

"If this guy is walking in circles, I'm gonna use this machete on him," said Vic with a grin.

Brad shook his head. "Go check on Kim.

I'm going to refill our canteens."

With a nod Vic headed off in Kim's direction, tossing his canteen back to Brad as he did. Catching it with one hand, Brad grinned and then pivoted, walking towards the stream he could hear running through the dense tree line. He made it a few paces before there was a sharp pinch in his upper left shoulder. At first he thought the mosquitoes had finally decided he would be good pickings. It wasn't until three more sharp pinches happened on his back that he looked over his shoulder to find small red darts protruding out of his skin.

The few seconds it took to register what he was seeing and what was happening was all it took for whatever had been in the darts to work. Brad's vision dimmed and his head swam. He swayed and was powerless to stop himself from falling forward into the black abyss of nothingness.

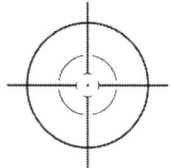

Chapter Two

Months later...

Alice Gladden leaned against the wall of the fraternity house chapter room, soaking in the sexual energy surrounding her. The party was in full swing and the place was busting at the seams with lust. It was just what she needed. She was starving, and not for food.

She'd spent most of the evening helping her best friend and college roommate, Mae Bertelot, get ready for a blind date. It had taken all of Alice to keep an even façade during it all, the need to feed gnawing at her from the inside out. Mae didn't understand what it was like to have a burning hunger. A need so insatiable that nothing seemed to satisfy it. Mae tended to frown upon what it was Alice needed to feed from—sex or sexual energy. Her succubus side demanded as much. It was a case of do so or die. No two ways about it.

Alice was often less than forthcoming about her needs in order to avoid having to see the pity and shame on her best friend's face. As far as Mae was concerned, Alice didn't need actual, full sex to handle her hunger—she only required energy. That was a lie. She needed both. The party would help check each box. It would give her both energy and full sex.

The fraternity party was packed full of exactly what she required. Hormone-driven young adults in their sexual primes too preoccupied with the shot at getting laid to notice her soaking in their lust. Her hunger was so deep that she couldn't have pretended to be casual about feeding it. The energy settled against her skin and seeped through her very pores, rejuvenating her—nourishing her.

The euphoric feeling was so great that she had to concentrate to keep her mental wards up to avoid listening in on everyone's thoughts around her. If she wasn't careful, the thoughts would all bombard her and she'd end up as sick as she'd have been without bothering to feed.

It wouldn't be the first time.

It had taken her years of practice to perfect the skill of blocking other people's thoughts, but she'd managed. At least with humans. Supernaturals were something altogether different. It was harder for her to control that particular *super power* around them.

She laughed softly as she thought of super powers. Mae didn't exactly love how Alice described what they could do. The ability to mock her circumstances was another coping skill Alice had acquired as a young girl. Even with adoptive parents who were supernaturals, she didn't feel like she fit in. Her mother was part vampire and part Fae and her father was a full-blooded were-cat shifter. Alice was none of those things. At least she didn't think she was. From what everyone could tell, she was mostly succubus. None of the doctors she'd been taken to while young were able to pinpoint all of what she was. They could only say for sure that she had succubus DNA in her make-up. Though, all of them agreed she was more than a mere succubus. Their inability to identify her genetic make up had been concerning to her adoptive parents and Alice. Basically, no one knew exactly what the hell she was.

Always comforting.

A hot mess, that is what I am, she thought with a sardonic smile. That was only half-true. Since meeting Mae, Alice had been making small strides to get her life in order. Baby steps, but steps all the same.

Music pumped through the air, the song choice one she didn't much care for. Her music choices always surprised others as they were not ones anyone would expect a woman her age to have. She could listen to Marvin Gaye for hours and never tire. So much soul and passion. The rubbish coming from the speakers in the fraternity was a far cry from the legendary Mr. Gaye.

The lights were dim, save two disco lamps someone had plugged in at opposite corners of the large room. The strobe effect the lights created was nauseating. Not to mention the entire room was tacky beyond belief. College-aged men had been left in charge of the decorating. That much was evident by the copious amount of light-up beer signs, centerfolds pinned to the walls in place of artwork, and numerous unidentifiable stains in the carpeting. She noted the lack of any textbooks to be found when there was an overabundance of girlie magazines scattered about the varying crates and boxes that were acting as end tables. Yes, college guys had certainly been the designers of the room.

It was nothing Alice would have subjected herself to if it wasn't absolutely necessary.

Unfortunately, she had to feed her succubus side and this was the best option. The alternative would leave her waking up with a man or men she didn't know, possibly several campuses or states away.

It had happened before.

It would probably happen again.

Each time she woke to find herself in the arms of men she didn't know, or remember being with, another piece of her soul died. Frustrated realization sank over her as the knowledge that this was her reality, her life, and it would be this way forever hit her hard.

She sighed, disliking her body's needs. While others required food and water to live, she needed sex or at the very least sexual energy in addition to normal basics in order to survive. The sexual energy felt like static in the air, crackling, alive, zapping around the room like a live current. The energy built around her, gathering in close like a protective blanket, warming her body, soaking through her skin, rejuvenating her. The more energy around her, the faster she warmed and felt full. But Alice knew to push beyond what she wanted and to store as much as she could. She'd been working hard to try to train her body to go longer and longer between full feedings. She was up to nearly a week now, which was saying something.

There had been a time she could barely make it through an entire day. She winced, no longer wanting to remember those times in the past. She wanted to focus on the here and now. The party was slamming, and she was getting what she needed. In addition, Mae was on a blind date. It was high time the girl lived a little. So what if the date was set up by Mae's mother. It was a red-blooded male, and Mae was in serious need of one of those. The girl had been spending way too much time in the art studio on campus sculpting her version of hotness. There was no denying the sculpture was sexy, but there was no replacing the real thing.

Alice's succubus side, or inner harlot as she'd affectionately termed it some years ago, stirred more, purring deep within her like a well-fed cat. It would still make room for a hot and hard male. Her succubus was an unabashed whore and seemed damn proud of it all. If only Alice could hold her head as high as her succubus wanted her to.

She took a long breath in and let additional energy seep in from the couples around her. They were too busy with one another to notice she was alone and quickly turning into a wallflower. That was fine by her. The guys weren't really her type. She preferred her men to be alpha, rugged and commanding. None of the young men present looked like they'd know how to tame a woman in the bedroom if their lives depended on it. They looked more like they were excited to just be close to women.

They probably were.

She snickered.

The place was jam-packed with horny people, each jockeying for the attention of another. She'd never really thought of herself as studious, but now that she was a fifth-year senior at the university and close to getting her degree, she found she looked forward to learning something new every day. She wasn't quite the bookworm her best friend Mae was, but Alice had started to develop something of a healthy respect for learning.

Though, she doubted that anyone spotting her at the party would think she was doing much more than having a good time. Actually, she was doing far more than that, but no one, other than Mae, knew the truth. Her succubus side wasn't something she was proud of. In fact, there were times she was downright ashamed of it and herself, but there was no changing what she was. No giving up the need to absorb sexual energy on a regular basis and so far, no giving up the need to fully feed the beast. She'd kept that part from Mae, knowing her friend would frown upon Alice sleeping with so many men. Mae prided herself on having held tight to her virginity and not giving in to society norms. Alice was jealous of that, of Mae being able to save herself for the right man. Alice had never had that luxury.

Nature had seen to that. It had stripped her of her options. As much as she wanted to be selective and wait for that perfect someone who made her feel whole, she didn't get that choice. The best she could hope for was that she could at least stomach the person come morning who would need to fill the full sex side of her hunger.

Her first sexual encounter nearly killed a guy. She had been fourteen, and it had been nothing more than heavy kissing, but she'd drained him. He'd been human, and no one knew then about her requirements. That she was powerful enough to harm another with what was essential to her survival. The boy had been left hospitalized for several months, in a coma, the human doctors at a loss as to what had caused his condition. Thankfully,

Alice's father had managed to pull some strings, and he had someone sneak into the facility after hours with a small dosage of vampire blood. It was low enough in quantity that the boy had never been at risk of turning, but the blood had sped his recovery.

Alice's guilt over who and what she was started then and it had never gone away. Ever since she'd tried her hardest to seek out supernatural males to fill her needs, but they were harder to come by than one would think in the college setting. So, she made do with what was available.

She glanced around the party and leaned against a wall, wanting to avoid sitting on any of the second-hand furniture for fear of getting something. No one in attendance piqued her interest or stirred her inner harlot's desires. Slim pickings for sure.

This is what I've been reduced to, trolling frat parties for food.

Self-loathing crept up on her, but she

pushed it down, hiding it in the recesses of what she feared would be a heart that was unable to heal. Unable to ever open and love another.

She let out an exasperated breath.

It was what it was, and she'd been forced to find ways to fill the void that didn't involve sleeping with a new man every other night. While she wore a smile whenever it happened, it was fake, born out of a need to protect her feelings. She was thought of as a wild child, and in many cases she fit the bill, but more and more she wanted to shed the image and be thought of as more than just the girl who was always with a new man.

The couple nearest her were lip-locked. The man's hands roamed up and under the woman's shirt as they moaned into each other's mouths. The guy fumbled around, looking awkward and confused as to what to do next.

Yep, hardly an alpha in the bunch.

If it wasn't for the sexual energy radiating

from them, Alice would have walked away to find a more titillating couple to stand near. This pair were merely eating each other's faces, not moving into foreplay.

She tsked, sure this was one of the reasons the saying that youth was misspent on the young had come to be. She could teach them a thing or two—okay, ten. With a small snort, she looked in the direction of two women trying their best to gain the attention of a tall, built male. He was a new arrival, and the minute Alice laid eyes on him the hair on the back of her neck stood on end. The man was good looking, no doubt about that. But there was something about him that seemed hard, removed from all that was happening around them.

The bitch better show tonight.

She stilled as the man's thoughts hit her hard. Her nostrils flared and she slowed her breathing, knowing better than to tip him off that she was hearing him mentally. It was rare for a human to get through her defenses. She concentrated on her personal walls and continued to watch the newcomer.

These fucking pussies don't know which end of a woman is up, he thought.

While she agreed, her inner alarms sounded, but she stayed in place, watching him, getting the sense he was more than merely human.

Much more.

He sneered as he raked his gaze over a group of girls entering from the other direction. He paid close attention to their backsides as they walked past him.

They'd be fun to break, he thought.

She gasped, feeling the full weight of the truth behind his words. The man wanted to inflict pain, and from the hardness in his eyes, he'd done just that before. She stiffened and eased off the wall, keeping a close watch on him. With slow movements, she pulled her cell from her back pocket, hoping to avoid drawing attention to herself. She was careful to control her breathing and heart rate to the best of her ability. If he was a shifter, and her instincts said he was, he could easily pick up on differences in her breathing and pulse. That tidbit she'd learned from her adoptive father and his friends.

Her father had spent his life pretending to be human, having to reinvent himself every so many decades to throw suspicion off the fact he didn't age. He, like many supernaturals, went so far as to alter his hair to try to make it look as if he was getting grays. Her father's current position was in the government. In truth, he'd been working for them for decades under different aliases. Currently, he was a face for the supernaturals, a representative for them within the government. A select few knew the truth about him.

Most didn't. And no humans knew the truth of him or their kind. And for good reason. Humans had a longstanding history of panicking and trying to kill that which they did not understand.

Dumbasses.

She pressed the contact button on her phone and selected the one for her father. She didn't dare risk dialing him. The supernatural male in the fraternity house with her would hear her conversation regardless of how low she tried to speak. Instead, she decided to type a message to her father.

Nile better have the fucking artsy bitch or I'm gonna rip his head off for leaving me to get this one, the man pushed out with his mind, agitation coating his every word.

The artsy bitch? Alice froze as fear danced up her spine. Images of Mae played in her mind and she lost her battle with controlling her breathing. She knew better than to lose her cool, but she couldn't stop the fear rising in her.

Mae is on her date with Corbin, she thought, calming herself. This guy was just a jerk and was probably all bluster, no real bark. Though, she did wonder who Nile was and who the artsy girl was he was supposed to pick up. Her inner alarms had more than likely gone off because he was a supernatural and she'd not run into many on campus outside of herself and Mae. Well, that and he was a douche. That much was clear from his thoughts.

This party is a joke, the man continued from his spot across the large chapter room.

Alice wondered what he was doing at a party known campus-wide to be a sexual haven if he didn't want anything to do with it at all. The more she watched him, the more unease returned, settling deep in her. She held her phone loosely, the text to her father started but never finished or sent.

The man raked his gaze around the room and then froze as his eyes landed on her. A sick, twisted smile tugged at his lips as he pushed off the wall, boldly walking in her direction. The college kids naturally made way for him, parting as if they too sensed the alpha in the male and subconsciously recognized how deadly he was.

Alice felt like a trapped rat, nowhere to run, nowhere to hide. He'd set his sights on her and he was headed straight for her.

Run, she thought, yet couldn't seem to get her feet to cooperate. By the time she managed to get her act together, he was close enough to touch her. The minute his hand made contact with her skin, her succubus screamed. Even the harlot didn't want the man's touch. When *she* wasn't on board with a guy, there was a serious problem.

She jerked out of his grasp, and he laughed, leaning in close, his hot breath moving over her cheek. "I can smell it on you."

She tensed. What could he smell on her?

"Succubus," he said with a hushed whisper, grabbing her arm again, squeezing tight. "We heard a rumor there was one in the area. Looks like the grapevine was right for once."

Alice found her nerve and stepped back, narrowing her gaze on the man. She looked him up and down and shook her head. "Not interested, bucko."

He smiled, but it never reached his eyes. His thoughts came at her in fragments. What he wanted to do to her had very little to do with sex. He let her leave his space, and she seized the moment, rushing down the hall and out of the front door. The cool night air rushed over her, giving her a sense of security. She walked at a brisk pace, nearly running in hopes to put distance between herself and the man. She exhaled, assuming she'd managed to put enough space between them to be safe. Something pinched her neck and she swatted at it, coming away with a small red dart. Confusion knitted her brow as she stared at the dart in her hand. Everything around her blurred and she staggered, turning and catching sight of the man from the party. He was there, holding a weapon in his hand as he wore the same, calculated smile he'd had on his face inside. The smile was the last thing she saw before darkness swallowed her whole.

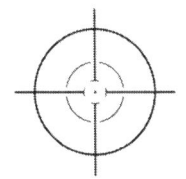

Chapter Three

Brad hissed as the guards took turns hitting him with chains. Each strike cut deeper, ripping flesh and drawing blood. He trembled in pain at the bite of each strike but did his best to avoid showing as much. He'd rather die than allow them to see they were getting to him. They were winning. It wasn't as if he could fight back. Not with the amount of drugs they had in his system and the fact he was tethered to the wall by silver-coated chains that also cut into his flesh. As a shifter he had a natural-born allergy to silver, and the guards exploited it to their advantage as often as possible. It would take him days to heal the damage they'd done already by chaining him the way they had.

In the past, they'd left him chained and bound overnight, and by morning the flesh, in the areas the silver-coated chains had touched, was totally gone, as was some muscle. That had taken Brad nearly a week to recover from before the doctors had commenced with a new set of testing. The testing had left his body changing, his body and his wolf's reactions to things differing and inconsistent. Worst of all, when he'd been forced to shift, his wolf form had increased in size. Not that it had been lacking in size prior to the testing, but now it was much bigger than the average shifter male wolf form. And more powerful. Much more powerful. In addition to it all, the wolf was now even more unpredictable.

Less trustworthy.

He'd never fully trusted the damn thing to begin with. Now he lived in fear of it. Fear of it taking over and leaving him trapped in wolf form for the rest of his days. He'd seen others who were being held have that happen. Hell, he'd even spent time stuck in shifted form during his period in captivity. The guards had loved that, loved taunting his wolf.

"Nothing else to say, you piece of shit?" demanded a guard as he hit Brad with a chain. This guard was relatively new but had come in with a chip on his shoulder. He wanted to show he was as hardcore as the others. That meant he was proving to be one of the more brutal in the mix. "Not so big and bad now, are you?"

The man wiped blood from his nose. Brad grinned, knowing he'd probably broken the guy's nose only a minute prior when he'd head-butted him. A different guard whipped him with another chain, bringing yet another hiss of pain from Brad in the process.

The guards would never have had the nerve to attack him if he wasn't chained and drugged. He'd have ripped them to shreds and they knew it. Hell, he had killed a number of them since his capture, however long ago that was.

Lifting his head, he glared at Albin, the leader of the guard group who seemed to take the most pleasure in his torture. Albin's beady blue eyes settled on Brad, and he smirked, showing off a row of teeth Brad wanted to knock out of the man's head. He also wanted to mount the guy's head on his front door, but that was neither here nor there.

"Like that, wolf?" Albin demanded, his rank breath moving over Brad.

Brad managed to lift his middle finger, despite barely being able to move. "Fuck off."

Albin's gaze heated. He lashed out again, hitting Brad in the face with the chain. "Scream, Durant. Scream!"

Growling, Brad continued to glare at Albin as he hung limply from the chains. They were secured to the wall and that was the only reason Brad wasn't currently on the floor—again. He'd been beaten so severely he wasn't able to stand on his own. Not yet anyway.

Albin whipped him again and tossed his head back, laughing with his buddies about the amount of blood they were drawing. They each took another turn, beating Brad more. Brad shut off to the pain, all while ignoring their comments and mocking. He focused on what he would do to them the moment he was able to gain the upper hand. He would make their deaths slow and painful. He'd make them suffer like they'd never suffered before. He'd make them pay for what they'd done to Vic. How they'd tortured his friend until he was nothing more than a broken shade of the man he used to be. They'd inflicted so much damage on Vic that Vic had been taken out of his cell on a stretcher, and Brad had never seen him again.

He was probably dead.

And Kim? She'd been taken as well, and while he'd been in the same location as her to start with, all that had changed quickly. He had no idea if she was alive or not either, or what she might have had to endure at the hands of the enemy.

Brad's gut twisted at the thought. Yes, his face would be the last the guards would ever see in this world. He'd make sure of that much for Vic and Kim, and for all the others the guards had hurt.

"Food break," said Albin, nudging the man nearest him. He dropped his chain and the others followed, doing the same. "I worked up an appetite."

Brad was starving but didn't dare hope for food. The meals he was given were barely edible and almost always laced with drugs. He'd learned long ago the medication they slipped in his food and drink was created to keep him sedated for the most part, and sometimes horny. So horny that he'd wanted to fuck a hole through the cement walls. It took resolve unlike any he'd ever known before to hold tight to the sexual urges when the scientists forced them on him.

They'd tried to get him to breed with various females they'd brought in, but he'd held out. Just barely, but he'd managed. He wasn't sure how much longer he could go before he broke. The last two women had been close calls. They, like the other females the doctors had administered drugs too, couldn't handle the meds. The women had died in his arms, despite his best efforts to try to save their lives.

I'm in hell, thought Brad coolly. The knowledge that he was resigned to his fate jarred him. He wasn't a quitter, but had to admit the fight was close to being beat out of him.

Albin slammed the cell door behind him, and his laughter echoed down the hall. Brad exhaled and closed his eyes, doing his best to catch sleep where he could. He needed the rest to heal the damage Albin and his buddies had done, and he wasn't sure when they'd be back.

They might lose interest in him for the rest of their shift, or they might very well devise even more devious ways to torture him while on their lunch break. One never knew with them.

As he hung by the chains, he started to drift off to sleep. While his mind was on the very edge of giving in to much needed rest, his thoughts became jumbled. There was a flash of long red hair and creamy pale skin and the overwhelming sense of fear washed over him, though it wasn't his own. It was someone else's fear.

A woman's.

Brad struggled against his holds as the visions continued to come to him. He couldn't make out the woman's face or too many clear details, but the smell of fresh strawberries and mint filled his head. The combination of scents gave him a burst of energy that seemed to center in his lower region. After the beating he'd taken, he wasn't sure how his dick still managed to get hard, but it did.

He opened his eyes slightly, seeing that he was still in his cell, still chained to the wall, and then his head fell forward, the visions continuing. He saw the pale, leggy redhead being lifted by a man he didn't know, but he could clearly see the guy's face. It was a face he wanted to etch into his memory. This man had caused the woman's fear and confusion. And this man wanted to harm the female.

"No!" Brad roared, jolting and making the chains rattle. At the same moment the vision and feeling of borrowed fear vanished, so did the smell of strawberries and mint. He instantly mourned the loss, and for the briefest of seconds he thought back to a time before he'd been held prisoner, when he used to daydream about what it would be like to have a woman of his own and a family.

There was a loud boom from the outer area. He jerked his head up, listening, his nose filling with the smell of smoke. A piece of him hoped the place was about to burn down and take him with it. Death by fire was welcome to death by slow torture.

When the door to his cell blew inward, the tiniest surge of hope filled him. Help had finally arrived. As men in masks burst in, carrying firearms and tranquilizer guns, he had a split second to wonder who they might be when one of them lifted a tranq gun, aimed it at Brad and fired several times, loading him with even more drugs.

"Grab the merchandise and let's go," one shouted as Brad fought to stay awake.

Not friendlies, he thought, fading away.

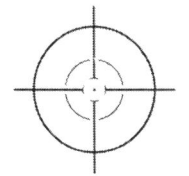

Chapter Four

Alice came up and off the hard floor with a quickness that surprised her, especially since it felt a lot like she'd been asleep for weeks and was possibly hit by a truck while she was out cold. The action was too much too soon. She swayed and fell, hitting the ground forearms first. Pain shot through her arms and her upper back, leaving her gritting her teeth. Her long hair fell forward over her face, and she took several deep breaths through her nose, trying to fight the urge to vomit, while her head and body were wracked with a combination of pain and something else.

What the heck happened?

Why did it feel as if she'd spent the night prior drinking to the point she forgot her own name? She looked to her side, half-expecting to find a man or rather men she didn't know, naked and near her, a clear sign she'd lost control—again—of her succubus. But no. She was alone and she wasn't in a bed.

Far from it.

She was on concrete ground. Either she'd had one hell of a night of partying or something was amiss. Her mind raced, trying to make sense of what was happening. The last thing she remembered was leaving the fraternity house and then something had stung her neck.

"No," she said softly, her voice a hoarse whisper, adding to the feeling of having been out partying too much the night prior. She moved to her hands and knees, worried she'd be sick at any moment if she didn't. Breathing slowly through her nose didn't help. The smell of the area she was in was heavy with mold and a scent she couldn't identify. It took a bit to calm her stomach. The wave of nausea subsided enough to try to focus more. As she did the reality of her situation hit her hard.

"I didn't get stung," the words came out harsh and scratchy, as if she'd spent the night before screaming.

It had been a dart she'd pulled from her neck. Everything had gone blank after that. She concentrated more and an image of the man who'd set her on edge from the fraternity party came to mind. The one with the empty eyes and the thoughts she'd found difficult to block.

A sick feeling settled in her stomach as she lifted her head slowly, taking in her surroundings. Bare cement block walls, crowding her in a space that couldn't have been more than eight by eight. There was a thick, rusty metal door before her. Long gashes were gouged in it, just under a window section that had bars in place of glass.

Alice pushed to her feet, this time slowly. It

took her a moment to understand the gashes were claw marks. Someone had tried to escape the room before. She wasn't the first person to be held in the cell. Somehow that did little to set her mind at ease. She reached for her phone in her back pocket only to realize it was gone. Of course it was.

What self-respecting criminal would leave her with a way to call for help?

She grunted and then patted herself down quickly, assessing if she was injured. There were long, dark bruises on her arms and her torso. It looked as if she'd been lashed or bound.

Absolute clarity came over her as she realized what the marks were from—a chain. Suddenly, a pang of sadness hit her hard, the feeling not for herself, but for someone else, though she wasn't sure who. All she did know was someone had been beaten severely and it was someone close to her.

From the looks of it, she'd been struck as

well.

The clothing she'd been wearing at the party was missing, replaced by a dark gray tank top and a pair of teal-colored bottoms that reminded her of something a doctor or nurse would wear. Her sandals were gone as well. She was left standing in her stocking feet on the hard concrete floor. Her mind ran every scenario it could think of as to why her clothing was missing; none were good.

There was no way to tell how long she'd been unconscious, or what had happened to her during it all, but the rising need to feed her succubus side soon indicated a good deal of time had passed or her body had suffered trauma. Both would require her to nourish her succubus side and soon. The sick feeling in her stomach returned at the idea of being left no choice but to feed from the asshole from the party, who she strongly suspected was behind her being in the cell.

She'd rather go hungry.

And she might if no one came.

The only positive to it all was that if that part of her needed to feed it meant no one had touched her sexually without her permission. So far that was the only light in her otherwise dark situation.

There was a small drain in the center of the floor and the surrounding floor level sloped towards it. She'd seen enough horror movies to know how drains in the floors of screwed up cells ended. As her mind raced with all the reasons there might be a drain there—none of them good—she bit back the urge to panic, to allow all sense of reason and rational thinking to abandon her.

Losing her mind wouldn't help matters. She had to keep her wits about her, figure out where she was, why she was there and better yet, how to escape. She made her way to the door and did her best to see if there was any weak spot. Even a hinge that she could possibly pry loose. There was nothing. When that failed, Alice searched all the corners of the cell, hoping to find a way to break out or something she could use as a weapon should the person holding her return.

She stilled as she thought about both scenarios. The person returning and what would happen if they never did. Neither outlook was one she wanted to face. Every ounce of her wanted to curl into a ball and cry, but she was stronger than that. Her father liked to say her hair color matched her temper—fiery.

Returning to the door, she pushed and pulled to no avail, but that didn't stop her. She put her fingers to the gash marks and had to calm herself when she realized the person held before her who had left them had her sized hands.

A woman's hands.

She gulped.

What kind of sick rabbit hole had she fallen down? And worse yet, what was yet to come?

The door to the cell opened and the jerk who had been at the fraternity party entered, looking altogether too pleased with himself. "Getting comfy, lil' succubus?"

She tensed.

He made a move to come at her and she scrambled backwards, wanting to avoid being any closer to him than she already was. His laughter echoed around the cell, grating on her nerves.

Another man entered the cell behind him, this one even taller than the other, but pale. Very pale.

Her succubus did its version of a hiss, warning her not to try to feed from the newcomer. There was something very wrong with him. His skin had a grayish hue to it and looked clammy. He eyed her for a second and then looked to the man from the party. "Bart, Felix wants the samples the lab took of this one hand-delivered to him at his place. He has plans for her."

Bart? The jerk who took her was named Bart? Figures. And what samples?

Bart's lip curled. "He's had a hard-on for getting a succubus back through the doors for years now, Nile."

Nile shrugged. "I stopped trying to figure out why. Do you want to run the samples over or should I?"

"Have Ezra do it," said Bart, his disturbing gaze never leaving Alice.

She swallowed hard, already knowing she didn't want to be left alone with him. And who was Ezra?

Nile paled more, if that was even possible. "*You* tell Ezra."

Bart squared his shoulders. "Dragon shifters don't scare me."

"Well, they do me," added Nile, wiping sweat from his brow.

Bart looked him over as if he was smelling

something that had gone bad. "I told you not to let those scientists do any tests on you."

Nile took a shallow breath. "They said they'd make me stronger and faster."

Sniffing, Bart curled his lip more. "They put some vampire in your makeup. Now you smell like you're rotting from the inside out. I think you're rejecting what they did. I warned you."

Nile's gaze lowered. "They said they can fix it."

Snorting, Bart faced the other man. "And you believe them? Fuck, look at the concoctions they spit out of this place. I wouldn't let them treat a common cold let alone test on me."

Nile glanced at Alice again, but didn't look away, his gaze settling on her in a way that left her feeling even more uneasy than she already did. His tongue darted out and over his lower lip in a suggestive manner, and her succubus hissed again.

Bart laughed. "You need to go feed. There are extra humans in the end cell. They're all lumped together. I grabbed some for Felix in case he comes by. Just pick from the girls. You know how he prefers to feed from men."

Nile nodded, but didn't look away from her. The more he fixated on her, the more her succubus reacted violently within her. "I could just take a small sample from this one."

Bart put a hand on Nile's chest. "No can do. Felix wants her for some reason. Mark her up and he'll end you and me both. Trust me, I want her too, but not to eat. Well, not to feed from, that is."

Even Alice's succubus wanted to be sick. The inner harlot didn't want anything to do with Bart or Nile, and Alice was on board with that. Suddenly, the college guys seemed very appealing in comparison.

Nile pointed to her arms. "She's already all marked up. Did you hear about what happened?"

Bart eyed her slowly. "Bitch started sprouting bruises and whip marks on her while she was sedated in the infirmary room. Thank the gods the cameras in there were on and recording or Felix would have killed me. He'd have thought I did it. But I didn't touch her. No one did."

"I heard she was crying out for some guy," said Nile. "That true?"

"I don't know. Yeah, I guess. I was more worried about Felix than what she was mumbling. Something about unchaining some guy and leaving him be. I don't know. Bitch is crazy."

She soaked in all of what they were saying. She'd really just had bruises appear on her at random while she was out cold? Who would she have been crying out for? She didn't know anyone who was chained up. Did she?

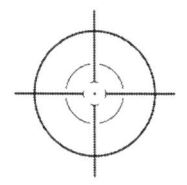

Chapter Five

"Yeah, eat me, jerk!"

Ezra sighed as he heard one of the newer arrivals antagonizing one of the other guards again. The spitfire redhead who had been brought in nearly two weeks back was proving to be more trouble than not for those trying to hold her. Ezra liked that about the young woman, liked that she gave as good as she got, but it would undoubtedly be what would get her killed. If she continued to cause such a fuss and stir, she'd suffer an "accident" at the hands of the guards. Oh, the guards would make it look like it was unavoidable and had nothing to do with them, but everyone knew the truth.

They might be reprimanded by the vampire in charge, or they might not. It would depend on the man's mood.

Ezra had seen the men who worked with him pull the stunt on more than one occasion. Normally, it was with male prisoners. Since he'd gone deep undercover with the organization, this was a first time Ezra could recall a woman being such a problem for the men. At least that he'd been made aware of.

He'd have laughed if he wasn't so concerned for her well-being. He'd overheard two of the guards talking about what they planned to do to her as soon as they got some alone time with her. The men were perverted and the stronger of the two, Bart, was obsessed with the redhead. Nile, the sickly vampire who palled around with Bart, pretty much just wanted to use the woman as a blood bank.

While Ezra's mission was to gather information on the underground supernatural trafficking rings and do nothing to stop the activity, he couldn't let the woman — Alice — be subjected to the whims of Bart and Nile. They were two of the more vile creatures he'd met since being pulled into this current bad-guy fold.

Ezra couldn't risk his cover or the mission by reaching out to his contacts for help. Too much was at stake. The information he was collecting would help to bring down some of the major rings, but not if the ring leaders packed up camp and ran, or if they killed him first. Either was possible if he risked his cover.

Alice was unique. Ezra's first encounter with her had been several days after she'd been brought in. Felix, the vampire who ran this particular trafficking ring, had been on the hunt for a young succubus. Ezra had first assumed the man wanted to sell her, as he did nearly every supernatural brought in. He'd hold secret auctions, and sometimes all of the bidding was done via the internet, the buyers viewing what they were bidding on by web camera only. Other times Felix would host a large-scale auction event where all the attendees were dressed in their best, fancy foods were served, and it felt like a wonderful night out. All except for the fact that men and women were brought in, often in cages on wheels, to be sold to the highest bidder.

The entire thing sickened Ezra.

After learning Alice was far more than just another succubus, Ezra found out Felix had bigger plans for her. The vampire intended to try to breed her, hoping to gain multiple subjects to auction off, rather than just one. He fucking hated Felix and every bastard who worked for him. Well, everyone except Caesar who was also an undercover agent with PSI. Caesar was currently pulling shifts at one of the sister sites about an hour's drive from Ezra's facility. Both places held supernaturals against their will, but the other place wasn't filled to the brim with sicko scientists who got a thrill out of doing tests on the people brought in.

This one was.

In his capacity as a doctor, Ezra had been to medical school and had obtained some type of medical instruction, depending on the century, more times than he could actually recall in his immortally long life. But then losing count of the finer details on his life was par for the course with living as long as he had. It was necessary to reinvent himself every so many decades to throw off human suspicions. It didn't matter what invented persona he took, he always ended up back in the field of medicine in some form or fashion. He liked helping people and he hated what the sick bastards working for Felix did. Some of the scientists and doctors had been fired from an even worse place called the Corporation. That organization, independent from the one he was currently undercover with, was huge, their reach extending to all the corners of the globe. Their pockets were deep and their depravity was even deeper.

The very fact that the doctors working

with Ezra now had been let go for being too harsh, or too cruel for the Corporation spoke volumes to just how twisted the men were. Ezra hadn't let on he had medical training or was more qualified than any person in the entire ring. That wasn't his cover, nor the mission. His cover was a simple guard. One who happened to advance quickly, but a guard nonetheless. This left him, for the most part, powerless to stop the atrocities that happened in the labs.

Alice was up next. She was scheduled for insemination soon—that was if and only if she survived what Bart and Nile had planned for her. Unable to stomach the idea of losing anyone else to the bastards, Ezra pivoted and marched into a director's office. This one was in charge of who went where and who had what done to them.

He looked around, assuring he was alone, before he pulled up Alice's information on the computer. He removed the scheduled insemination information and changed it out with a transfer request to the sister facility Caesar was at. It wasn't freedom for the young redhead, but it would buy Ezra some time to formulate a way to get her out fully without putting his cover at risk.

He closed out everything on the computer and left the office, hoping no one had seen him. Walking with purpose, he headed in the direction of Alice's cell. He found a guard stumbling out of the room, cupping himself as he bent forward, tears in his eyes.

"What happened?" demanded Ezra.

The guard twisted and then expelled the contents of his stomach in the hallway. After several deep breaths, he looked up, his eyes rimmed with tears. "The bitch kicked me in the balls."

"And she'll do it again!" shouted Alice from her cell. "No means no, jerk."

Pleased Alice had defended herself, Ezra hid his smile and touched the guard's shoulder. "Head to the infirmary. I'll handle her. She's being transferred anyways."

The man nodded. "Good. She's fucking crazy."

Ezra bit back a laugh as the guard limped away. When he was sure the man was gone for good, he entered Alice's cell and found her with her arms crossed in front of her, her hip cocked to one side and an expression that said she was incredibly proud of herself.

Total trouble, he thought.

She winked. "Thanks."

He clucked his tongue on his cheek. "I assumed I'd managed to block your ability to read my thoughts."

She shrugged. "I hear it quieter in my head now, but it's not fully gone yet."

He'd been surprised the first time she'd let on about her ability to connect with others mentally. She'd read that he was working undercover and that he was unhappy with what he was witnessing. And she trusted him because of it.

She also possessed a good deal of Fae in her genetic makeup, as he discovered by reading her chart. The little troublemaker didn't realize it yet, but she was able to wield magik with the levels of Fae in her. Ezra wasn't sure he wanted to tell her. She was hard enough to handle as it was. They didn't need magik coming into play as well.

"Come on," he said, putting his hand out to her. "You're being moved."

She eyed him and then glanced around the room. "Something bad is going to happen and you want to try to move me to safety, right?"

"Alice?"

She stiffened. "If you're wondering if I got that from you mentally, no. I didn't. I put it together on my own. Bart and Nile don't know to block their thoughts from me, and trust me when I say they're planning to do something really bad."

His chest tightened. "I know. Come on. We

need to get you transported."

"I'll be there alone?"

The fear in her voice moved him. "No, kiddo, I'll find a way to stay close. Then we'll get you to freedom. Sound like a plan?"

"Thank you."

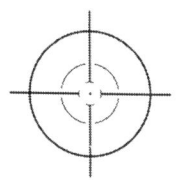

Chapter Six

Brad paced the cell that had become the newest in a long string of them, his body on edge. He was no stranger to being held prisoner. He wasn't sure of the exact timeframe that he'd been held in total, as he rarely saw glimpses of sunlight, or was able to track days, but it was probably a year — or close to it, since he'd been captured while on the trip in South America.

He'd played that fateful day over and over in his head during his time in captivity, always coming back to the same certainty. He'd been betrayed by Professor Krauss and he was pretty sure Vepkhia had been involved. Brad had to wonder if anything he and Vic had been told about PSI was real, or if the organization was simply made up to lure them into a false sense of security before grabbing them and testing on them.

He sighed.

The blame game would get him nowhere. It wouldn't change the fact he was a prisoner. That he'd been held in some form another for nearly a year. He felt like a trapped rat, stuck on a wheel with no hope of ever getting anywhere. There for scientists to view and mock at will, his fate in their hands. And most of them were sick bastards. They got off on inflicting pain and being sadistic pricks. When he'd found himself being yanked from the last facility by men in masks, he'd foolishly hoped it was a rescue mission.

He'd been wrong.

Nearly dead wrong.

He was back in the clutches of madmen, different ones, but mad all the same. He should have been used to it by now. Used to the constant prodding and poking. Used to guards who took great pleasure in being as brutal as possible.

Brad took in the bare walls surrounding him, feeling as if they were closing in on him. With a growl he spun and punched the wall, cracking the cement block slightly. He hit it again and again, making some headway, but not enough. He knew from practice that there was more than one layer to the holding cell walls. The facility had obviously been retrofitted with supernaturals in mind. And caging one required reinforced everything.

Brad drew his fist back, his knuckles bloody and raw. As quickly as the injuries had appeared, they vanished, his skin smoothing over. He wiped away the blood and there was no sign he'd been hurt.

Healing had been something he'd done quickly prior to his capture. Since he'd been subjected to test after test, procedure after procedure, he found everything that he'd once come to accept about himself was in question. He now healed at a rate that even supernaturals would find impressive. Though, there were some wounds that, while the scars had faded significantly, were still evident. He was also stronger than he'd been. But with great healing and strength came a huge weakness—control. His once semi-solid control over his wolf side was nearly nonexistent. Most of his time was spent trying to keep himself from shifting forms. Each period he did lose control and give in to the beast, he lost track of time and woke in a weakened state. And from the expressions on the scientists and guards' faces, he'd been a monster while shifted.

The fear of changing and not being able to return to human form was real and always with him. He'd seen other test subjects fall victim to it. Seen them enter their shifted form, only to remain stuck in it. The doctors and scientists performed even more tests before finally putting the test subject down and out of its misery.

I wish they'd put me down, he thought, lowering his gaze to his fists once more. They'd turned him into something. A monster. He'd end up like the others. He'd get stuck in wolf form before being shot execution style. It was just a matter of time. He could only hope they killed him sooner rather than later. Controlling the urges was getting harder and harder.

The sick sons-of-bitches had been trying to force him to mate from the word go. They tried just about anything they could think of in order to get him to take a woman, use her, spend his seed in her and give them what they wanted—more test subjects. He'd managed to resist it all so far, but his self-restraint was wavering. They kept pumping him with more and more of those fucking drugs and he knew he'd break soon enough. It didn't matter that a new puppet master pulled his strings, a bad guy was a bad guy. Shades of gray was the shit fairytales were made of and this was no fucking fairytale.

"If it is," he said softly, his attention moving to the cracked wall, "I'm the big bad wolf."

He paced the cell once more, his nerves on edge, heavy with worry for the newest subject they had wanted him to breed. Her name was Mae and she seemed like a nice enough girl. And he had *zero* sexual interest in her. That didn't mean anything in the world of the people holding him. The vampire who was in charge, or at least pretended to be in charge, was after the same results as the sick bastards who took him from South America. They all wanted more product to sell and test. And in this scenario Brad and the other test subjects were the product, the merchandise to do with as they may.

His thoughts returned to Mae. From the moment he'd heard her humming a soft melody for him, he'd felt somewhat calmer around her and he'd also begun to fear the inevitable. The moment when they'd shoot him up with even more drugs and force a partial or full change on him. He feared he'd do the unthinkable, and in that state force himself on her or rip her to shreds. Neither one was something he wanted to happen. Not to any woman, but seeing Mae in a sexual light seemed extra wrong for some reason he couldn't explain.

Didn't want to bother to try.

"Where is she?" he asked of the empty room. He'd become quite good at talking to himself since he'd been taken. Occasionally, someone listening in over the surveillance system would answer, nearly always being assholes when they did.

It seemed like hours since they'd taken Mae and he hadn't seen anyone else since then. He didn't want to think on what they were doing to her. He'd seen many women come and go since he'd been taken. For a while he'd desensitized himself from it all, but Mae had changed that for him. He felt a strange friendship forming with her. It wasn't attraction, but he did care about her and her well-being.

He heard footsteps and then smelled one of the guards. A snarl broke free from him and claws threatened to emerge from his fingertips. As his hate of his captors rose, he caught scent of something else. Something that didn't make him want to kill. Something that seemed very out of place in the holding facility.

Strawberries and mint?

What a strange combination. His wolf took notice of it as well, wanting to know the source. It didn't take long before his cock took a keen interest as well. He stiffened and tried to will his lower extremity into behaving. It had a mind of its own and currently it was thinking "Get bent, asshole, whatever is coming smells fuckable."

Blatantly, he reached down, took hold of himself through the hospital-issued scrub pants he wore, and adjusted. He found no relief in a new position. As the scent's strength grew, so did the urge to screw a hole through the wall. His body was pumped full of so many drugs that he feared he might give in and hump the cement blocks. Rage at his captors rushed over him at the same moment intense need slammed through him as the smell of strawberries and mint grew even stronger.

Looking through the display window into Mae's cell, Brad watched as the door to her room opened. It wasn't Mae who entered. A stacked, leggy redhead staggered in, her long hair falling forward, covering her face partially at first. The same need that had hit him at her scent, rushed through him even stronger, centering in his groin once more. With a groan, he held himself, hoping no one would notice just how much she turned him on. The people holding him were hell-bent on breeding the women, and Brad didn't want them to realize just how much the redhead appealed to him in that manner. For the briefest of moments, he actually had a flash in his mind of seeing her frame swelling with his child.

He had to shake his head to clear the image. As she flipped her long hair back, showing off just how stunning she was, all hope of him erasing the thought of having children with her was abandoned. Her gaze narrowed on the guard who had thrust her into the room. Nothing short of rage burned in her eyes.

"Hey, I told you that Ezra said to bring you to this cell," the guard said, lifting his hands in the air as if to show he was innocent in it all. "Stop looking at me like you want to rip my nuts off."

Brad's appreciation of the woman increased. Anyone who was willing to give the bastards holding them a hard time was all right by him.

"Oh, I do," she snapped, her voice making Brad's cock stir more. "I want to spoon feed them to you, asshole."

The guard nodded, his eyes widening. He made a motion to cover his groin area. "I know. Crazy bitch."

Hearing the man call her a bitch set Brad on edge. His wolf pushed up, wanting out, wanting to rip the guard's head off for daring to speak to the woman in such a way. He wasn't sure how long had passed before he got something close to control of his beast. The guard shut the cell door and the woman folded her arms under her large breasts, drawing more attention to them. Not that they needed any help in that department. She was extremely blessed.

He thought quickly of what it would be like to bury his head between her breasts as he sampled them with his lips, before moving down her slowly, tasting all of her.

"Dick!" she shouted at the closed cell door, jerking Brad from his sexual daydream.

He grinned, liking her fire.

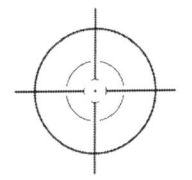

Chapter Seven

Alice adjusted her shirt and blew out a long, annoyed breath as she found herself in yet another holding cell. It was the fourth holding cell she'd inhabited since she'd been grabbed from her university campus while attempting to leave a fraternity party. She'd been terrified to start with, unsure where she was, who had taken her and why she'd been grabbed. Now she was pissed.

The guard who had dragged her to the newest cell was one she'd only just met since arriving at the current facility. Apparently, her previous guards had given the man an earful because he'd been leery of her from the word go.

Good.

She fought the urge to lift her middle fingers and tell this one to go fuck himself. The last guard she'd tried that with had hit her in the gut so hard she'd had trouble breathing for a couple of days. She was still a little tender but she wasn't going to let on. Giving them the satisfaction of knowing they'd caused her pain just wasn't in her personality.

The desire to tuck away and cry until she ran out of tears was still overwhelming, but she clung to her anger. It was the only thing keeping her going. The guard slammed the door as he left and she curled her lip in disgust.

When she was moved from the other holding facility, she'd been both terrified and hopeful. Foolishly, she'd thought she might be able to find the perfect opportunity to escape. That maybe Ezra would change his mind about the risk and just set her free. That hadn't been the case. Ezra had continued to play the part of dutiful guard, even though she knew he wasn't with them. He wasn't a bad guy. She couldn't say the same for the rest of the men.

She'd been shackled for her transport, a cloth hood put over her head, and for a portion she'd been carried. Mostly because she'd been kicking and hitting at the men trying to escort her out. The ride over had taken, by her estimate, an hour at most. She'd done her best to attempt to count turns and anything that might indicate the path they'd taken. She was fairly certain they'd driven over at least one, possibly two sets of railroad tracks, and on their approach she'd smelled the ocean and heard seagulls. The telltale sound of a boat blowing its horn had confirmed her suspicion that she was near docks.

It wasn't much, but it was something. She'd take anything that might help her figure out where she was and who, exactly was holding her. Befriending Ezra had proved somewhat useful, although it wasn't a total win, as she was still being held prisoner. His promise to get her out and to safety was one she wanted to fully believe in but she was skeptical. It wasn't that she didn't trust him, she didn't trust the situation and all the players involved. There were elements out of his control.

At least the new place was cleaner than the last. When they'd taken the hood off her, she'd noticed that much straight away. She looked around at what would be her new home, at least for now. It was bigger than the others. At least double the size and wasn't coated in mold.

I'm really moving up in the world, she thought with a snort.

Alice ran her hands through her long hair, pushing it back from her face as she turned slightly, studying her environment, hoping this cell had a weakness. It was built much like the others she'd been in, but this one had a thick viewing window and the viewing window wasn't showing her an empty cell. She froze as she spotted a man standing on the other side of it.

At first she thought he was a guard watching her, but from his disheveled appearance and scrub bottoms that matched her own, she surmised he too was a captive. A rather good-looking one at that, despite his overgrown beard and long, unkempt hair. His upper body was bare, showing off his toned frame, though he looked thinner than a man of his size and stature should be. That didn't take from his muscular build though.

Her inner harlot leapt with joy at the sight of the man and Alice nearly staggered from the force with which her succubus wanted her to know she'd accept that man fully. That there would be no resistance to him, no guilt, no second-guessing. Never had it behaved this way. Normally, the succubus seemed rather bored with the males she encountered, wanting only to use them to sate its baser needs. But this man was different. This man piqued her succubus's interest and her sexual desires. He made her cravings intensify to the point they hurt. She fought the need to double over from the cramp slicing through her. She'd suffered them before, but never this strong. Never this intense.

Alice wanted to blame it all away on the fact she'd been unable to properly feed since her capture, but her gut told her that wasn't the case at all. This was different.

Raw.

Primitive.

And focused solely on the man through the viewing glass. Her mouth went dry as quick flashes of what it would be like to have him above her, pumping in and out of her, swept over her. Her inner thighs quivered with lust. She wanted the window between them to shatter, just like she wanted her body to do when he brought her to climax—and she was sure he could. From the smoldering look in his dark brown eyes, he knew his way around the female form.

Part of her survival had always hinged on her being able to read people's sexual tells. The way they'd tip their head or bite at their lower lips, or the way they would clench a fist or change their posture when they were attracted to someone. His tells were so obvious they'd have knocked her over the head if they could. He was clenching his fists, his breathing rapid, his nostrils flaring, his pupils dilating. His gaze was focused on her mouth, another tell. She wet her lips and he squeezed his fists tighter.

Good.

That meant the fierce attraction wasn't one-sided. If she couldn't fight her succubus and its needs then maybe this man would be willing to help her. At this point she wasn't sure simple sexual energy would do, but she'd try it. She had to. There was no other choice in the matter. And if she didn't get a handle on it and soon, she'd do the unthinkable and use a guard—something she did not want to resort to. She'd never be able to wash that emotional stain away.

Ever.

Her attention remained on the man through the viewing glass. She visually traced every bit of his upper body she could see. She committed it to memory, each ridge of muscle making her want to reach down and touch herself. He was the type of man she could stare at all day.

Stop, she practically screamed at her inner harlot. *Focus on escaping, not jumping the man's bones.*

It had been too long since she'd fed that side of herself. Too long without sexual energy. Controlling the succubus wasn't going to be easy. Especially not with a hottie being housed in the room next to her.

Needing to cling to her composure, Alice kept her eye on him and spoke. There were so many things she wanted to say, but none of that came out. "Who are you?"

His hungry gaze intensified. "Brad. And you?" he asked, his voice deep and rich, only adding to the intense interest her succubus side had for him. Of course she'd be put next to temptation personified. Why not?

"Alice," she replied, swallowing hard. A glass of water would be great. Especially one that wasn't drugged, as were most of the ones she'd been given since her capture. She chanced another glance in Brad's direction and found him still staring at her, although he was now even closer to the window. This time his gaze was locked on her breasts. He bit at his lower lip and Alice held back a smile. She liked knowing he was attracted to her.

The need to ask him to strip off the thin bottoms, grab his cock and stroke it while she watched him masturbate was all consuming. It took all she had to refrain. She wasn't sure it would be enough or that she'd be able to cage her own inner beast once the succubus was given a taste of the man's energy.

She'd heard horror stories of what happened when her kind was denied for too long. Heard tales of how the person they chose to feed from in that state was left a husk—a dry, withered shell, appearing mummified in some respects.

She couldn't do that.

Not to him.

She'd have to figure out another way to sate her needs. She looked upwards at the ceiling, attempting to stare at anything other than his abs. If she could keep a tight hold on her succubus she just might make it through the night. Ezra had promised it wouldn't be long before he got her out. She just had to hold on to that hope for now.

Easier said than done.

She exhaled loudly and twisted, her attention pulled in the direction of the bed in the corner of the cell. She was about to make a smartass comment on how much more luxurious this set-up was than her last when she spotted a discarded pair of glasses lying on the bed. She knew those frames. She'd seen them enough in the last four and a half years.

They were Mae's!

She bolted in the direction of the bed, her heart hammering so loudly she couldn't hear anything over it. They had Mae too? She gripped the glasses in her hand tight enough to know they were real but not enough to break them. No. They couldn't have Mae.

"Who was in here before me?" she asked, desperation clinging to her every word as she stared at the window and Brad.

"That is Mae's cell," he said softly, confirming her worst fears. His nostrils flared, though this time she instinctively knew it wasn't with desire, but with rage and anger inferred. "They took her hours ago. She was having a reaction to the drugs they're giving us."

It took everything in Alice to hold tight to the tears wanting to come. She'd been locked up, threatened, beaten and tested on over the past however long she'd been held and nothing had brought her to the brink of breaking like hearing confirmation that Mae was a prisoner too. No help would be coming. No one would know she was missing. Her penchant for taking off for weeks at a time would mean her parents wouldn't suspect anything out of the ordinary. Only Mae would have questioned her absence. Mae would have sent up warning flags to others in their lives.

Maybe he was wrong.

She shook, clutching the glasses in one hand. "They have Mae too?"

"You know her?" he asked, surprise in his voice.

"She's my best friend," answered Alice, the fight and will to give them all hell rushing from her body. She sank to the floor and sat, holding the glasses to her chest. "She's so innocent and always forgetting things. She's not a fighter. She can't handle this."

"How long have you been here?" he asked, something off. His words didn't match his emotions, that was easy to pick up on.

She didn't respond at first, but when she finally did she knew she sounded tired. "At *this* facility, just today. I was at a different one for a couple of weeks. I think. Time is hard to keep without a clock." He nodded, as if he understood her struggle to figure out nights from days and how hard it was to keep an accurate count. "They said I was too difficult to deal with at the other place. They brought me here. Something about it being higher security or something."

A flicker of pride reflected back at her from him and she tipped her head, wondering why her confessions would cause him to fill with such an emotion. Her thoughts quickly returned to Mae. Alice knew what she'd endured at the hands of the people holding them. She couldn't imagine what her best friend had been subjected to. "Oh gods, they've had Mae this whole time, haven't they?"

Her succubus side continued to read his tells. While he still wanted her sexually, there was something else there. Was it genuine concern for her?

"She's been here just over two weeks. She mentioned being taken the night of a blind date."

Alice gasped and locked gazes with him. "I was taken then too."

She nearly lost her grip on her tears, nearly let them win. There was a loud creaking noise, followed quickly by the door to her cell opening. Relief rushed through her as Ezra entered the room. Desperation clung to her. She needed to feed and soon and she needed to find her friend.

"They have my friend Mae," she said, knowing her voice sounded weak.

Nodding, Ezra stepped into the cell more. "I know."

He'd known they'd had Mae all along? Her temper rose, chasing away the urge to cry and replacing it with the sudden need to throw something at the man.

"Why didn't you tell me?" she demanded, clutching Mae's glasses to her chest. "You came with me from the other place and you never once mentioned they have my best friend too?"

There was a level of sadness in his otherwise handsome face. "I only *just* found out this morning. I didn't know that two of you were taken from the same location. That information wasn't presented to me prior. She's fine, Alice. I promise."

She trusted him. She'd read his thoughts enough before he'd learned to block her to know he was a good man stuck in a bad situation. "Did they force her to breed?" asked Alice, feeling sick at the idea. "Like they threatened to do to me?"

The question drew a snort from Ezra and a violent outburst from Brad as he punched the window separating them, his entire body coiled with rage. He then flipped Ezra off.

Alice's eyes widened in surprise. He didn't know her, yet he was irate and ready to blow on her behalf.

Ezra chuckled, partially under his breath as he shook his head, his long hair moving about. "Relax, wolf. I'm only laughing because any man who tries to get near Alice has been very sorry."

She'd have taken offense but she was sort of proud of her reputation among the guards. She shrugged casually. "I told them they weren't touching me. They should have listened."

"Not sure the one you went at this morning will ever have use of his manhood again," said Ezra, grinning wide before he winked.

She smiled back. "Good. Asshole should know it's wrong to touch a woman who doesn't want to be touched. Now every time his dick doesn't work, he'll remember why that is."

Ezra held his hand out. "Mae needs her glasses. She's resting now and I made sure to leave someone with her who will keep her safe."

Alice stiffened, her gaze narrowing. "This Caesar guy you're working with?"

"The fact you were able to read my thoughts before I figured it out and started blocking you is unnerving," said Ezra. "And to answer your question, no. Caesar isn't with her. He's not checked in with me yet. He should have."

"You think something happened to him, don't you?"

Ezra offered a curt nod. "I have to say you're one of the few people in my long life who can do that—who can read me. I'm not really a fan of it."

Alice lifted her shoulders and let them fall slowly, trying to appear calm and collected.

She was neither. She needed to feed and soon. "Never met a guy who could shift into a dragon. Hell, I didn't think dragons were even real."

"Most people assume werewolves aren't real," replied Ezra. "And I think Brad would be the first to dispute that claim."

"I'm a lycan," he said, posturing.

Ezra glanced at him. "You're a hell of a lot more than just a lycan now after the Corporation got their hands on you and you know it."

"The Corporation?" he asked and then stepped back from the glass. "The people who took me to start with?"

Ezra nodded and spoke, "I was planted with them, in one of their German facilities to start with. It became clear I was needed on this end more."

Alice stepped closer to Ezra and handed him the glasses. "Tell Brad about the Shadow

Agent Ops thing."

Groaning, Ezra eyed her. "Announce it to everyone, why don't you, little succubus?"

She glanced at Brad. He was a prisoner too. "Like he's going to tell them. He wants them dead as much as me. Maybe more."

Ezra stared in Brad's direction. "I'm guessing much, *much* more, Alice. Brad has been held against his will nearly a year, at least from what I can tell by his paper trail."

Brad touched the glass, his expression softening somewhat. "Do you know about Vic or Kimberly?"

Ezra glanced at the door and then back to the window. "Vic is still being held by the Corporation. They have him buried deep in one of the black sites. I suspect they intended the same for you, but you were liberated from their holding station."

Alice tilted her head. What had Ezra meant by liberated?

Brad jutted out his chin. "I'm not going back."

"Didn't think you'd want to," said Ezra.

"Kimberly?" Brad asked, desperation showing on his face, and for a second a small pang of jealousy struck Alice, though she wasn't sure why. She had nothing to be jealous of. It wasn't like she and Brad were an item.

Ezra nodded. "Kimberly has been free for months. That is all I know. I've been in too deep to keep up on it all."

Exhaling, Brad put his head against the glass. He then drew in a deep breath and locked gazes with Ezra. "Get Mae and Alice out of here no matter the cost. Use me as a diversion if need be. I want them safe."

He'd been locked up already for how long, and the nimrod wanted to make a martyr of himself for her? Something deep inside her snapped. She would not allow harm to come to him, no matter the personal cost to herself. With the knowledge came her famous temper.

"You don't even know me. Why would you sacrifice yourself for me? Are you stupid?"

"I still want you safe."

Ezra stood tall. "I want *all* of you safe."

The door to the cell opened and a different guard appeared. "Ezra, we have a problem. Something is happening at the other facility. Felix has given the green light on Operation Red."

What was Operation Red?

She waited for additional information from the new guard but none came. From the expression on Ezra's face and his tense body language, Operation Red was far from a good thing. Ezra inclined his head in the man's direction. "Go to the main room. I'll be there in a minute. I'll deal with these two myself."

The guard left and Ezra grabbed Alice's arm. "Alice, you need to listen to Brad. Caesar isn't responding to my calls, and with what Felix ordered, I know something bad has happened to him." He looked to Brad. "Alice,

I'm going to trust Brad to get you out of here."

She stiffened. She was being put into the hot guy's care? There was no way she'd be able to control her inner harlot if she was making contact with Brad. She'd use him and dry him up like what had happened to the first boy she'd ever kissed.

No! She wouldn't let that happen.

Ezra kept his gaze on Brad. "I'm unlocking you. Can I trust you with her?"

"I'm not leaving this place without Mae," pushed Alice, wanting both her friend safe and distance to be kept between her and Brad. It was for his own good.

Ezra held her firmly. "An operative I trust is with her. I need to get there and make sure he's come out of the drugs given to him before any of these assholes decide to start the killings with him. The two of you need to get out. If Felix has Caesar, he'll find a way to break him. It's what he does. Caesar is strong, but not that strong."

Couldn't Ezra see she was on edge? That she was holding on by a thread? That her succubus was on the verge of doing something horrible to a good man? Digging her heels in, Alice tried to plant herself and remain in place. Ezra wasn't having any of it. He lifted her with ease and carried her from her cell and right to the door of Brad's cell. Alice's mind raced. She couldn't be close to him. Couldn't allow contact.

Ezra opened the door and set Alice down, giving her a good shove right into the arms of the man Alice feared touching most at the moment.

Brad.

"Take her and go."

For being locked up, Brad smelled great. Better than great. He smelled good enough to lick and her inner harlot wanted to do just that and more. Her succubus roared to life, wanting him, making heat flare throughout her body.

Ezra plucked the glasses from her hand.

"Mae will need these."

"I'm not leaving without my friend," pressed Alice, trying and failing to get out of Brad's grasp. His hands felt so good on her sexually starved skin that she nearly sank into his embrace, all while her mind wanted her to do the opposite. She could feel herself starting to draw upon his energy. She didn't want to hurt him. Didn't want to be what finally ended him when he'd clearly fought to survive for as long as he had. She opened her mouth to scream at the men and confess that she couldn't control her lust, when all of a sudden Brad lifted her and tossed her over his shoulder as if she were a sack of potatoes.

Cream flooded her sex and she nearly moaned, only just managing to hold it in. She clung to what little control remained over her succubus, drawing on her anger to try to keep Brad safe. The stupid fool was going to get himself killed trying to save her and she was going to be the weapon that ended him. She hit at his back to no avail. "Put me down!"

He stiffened and she felt it then, his desire for her rolling off him in waves. He spanked her bottom with two good swats, drawing a yelp from her. "Silence, woman. I'm getting you out of here."

Brad turned enough for her to see Ezra again. The dragon-shifter looked pleased. She wanted to hit him too.

Asshole.

Ezra spoke to Brad, "Left, right and then two lefts. An exit is there. I have a safe house not far from here." He gave the address and then cast a worried look at Alice.

She had to close her eyes to focus on keeping her succubus side under control. It wanted her to stop struggling and start trying to jump Brad's bones. It didn't matter that there was obvious danger around them and something big was going down. All it cared about was getting laid and it wanted Brad to be the man doing the dirty deed.

"Copy that," replied Brad.

He was a shifter. Couldn't he sense how much of a threat she was?

Worst shifter instincts ever, she thought, opening her eyes, staring at his tight ass from her position over his strong shoulder. *But best shifter ass ever.*

She was about to reach down and try to feel the ass she was so focused on when loud sirens, their sound was nearly deafening, began going off. Brad's entire body stiffened and he jerked, setting her down and then swaying. Something was wrong.

Very wrong with him.

She touched his shoulder, worry lacing her. "Brad?"

He bent, nearly going to one knee, his hands moving over his ears. It was clear he was in immense pain. The need to jump his bones subsided somewhat, as if her succubus was as worried about his safety as Alice was. She didn't know what to do or how to stop the noises that were obviously hurting him. She did the only thing she could think to do—she put her hands over his ears, and bent, locking gazes with him. The need to kiss him was there, yet she resisted, scared she'd reduce him to a dried-up shell of a man all while trying to help him. Instead, she continued to stare into his dark gaze, willing him to know she was there and she wasn't about to leave him.

There was movement at the end of the hall and at first she thought it might be Ezra. It wasn't. It was one of the asshole guards. She gasped and Brad came upright, growling loudly as he yanked her behind him in a protective manner. In the blink of an eye he was charging the guards, seemingly unconcerned with the fact several of them were carrying shock sticks. One of them rammed a stick into Brad and his body jerked but he didn't go down.

Holy crap!

Her man was alpha through and through.

My man? she thought, freezing for a moment at the shock of the idea of Brad being hers in any way. When she shook off the stunned moment of it all, she realized he was being converged upon from all sides by guards. Brad struck one and the man dropped his stick. Alice wasted no time snatching it up and thrusting it into the guard closest to her. The man not only jerked and went down, he started to drool too.

Yeah, her man was a total badass.

Stop with the my man *thing*, she scolded herself.

Brad twisted, his eyes wild as he glanced down at her holding the shock stick. From his expression he looked as though he thought she might actually use the thing on him. That was absurd. She was about to let him know as much when blood began to trickle from his nose. Worry slammed into her. She reached up, touching just under his nose. With a shaky hand, she held up her index finger that was coated in blood.

Brad shrugged, like it was no big deal he'd just sprung a leak from the nose. He grabbed her other hand and turned, heading in the direction they'd originally been going in. He practically dragged her along. She did her best to keep pace, but he was faster than she could ever hope to be. Huge pops and bangs sounded from what felt like all directions in the hallway. Brad whipped around and then slammed her into the unforgiving wall, pressing his powerful frame to hers, making her succubus shout with victory.

Her body was so starved for sex and sexual energy that at first she didn't realize what the noises had been. As Brad jerked several times and grunted, she understood. Someone was shooting at them and they'd managed to hit Brad more than once.

"You're bleeding!" yelled Alice a second before there was a massive explosion and heat and fire swelled around them.

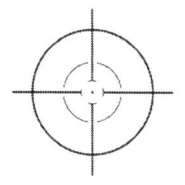

Chapter Eight

Brad's ears rang as he lifted his head, for a moment unsure where he was or who he was with. His head felt heavy and his body was hot, pain radiating throughout him. He tried to look around only to find his vision blurred to the point he couldn't make out anything. He touched his temple lightly, trying to think, to focus on what had happened. Slowly, it came back to him. He remembered trying to make a run for it with someone.

Who?

His heart hammered quickly in his chest as he recalled everything. Alice. He'd been trying to get her to safety. To freedom. Something had happened. He'd been so close to the exit. So close to freedom and then everything had turned on its axis. The world had shifted beneath his feet and it had felt as if someone had dropped a truck on him.

Not a truck, he thought. The building. The fucking building had exploded around them.

Frantic, he felt around his immediate area, still unable to see through the smoke, in search of Alice. His fingers skimmed over broken pieces of the building. He lifted a portion and squeezed, reducing it to dust nearly instantly, his emotions were so high. He took a deep breath in, hoping to at least catch her scent, but all he could smell was the aftereffects of the explosion and charred flesh. Panic continued to assail him. Had Alice been injured? Had she been killed?

"No!" he roared, the sound deep and visceral. The wolf pounded at him from within, demanding to be free to hunt for the woman. With nothing more than adrenaline guiding his actions, he put his palms to the floor and pushed up. He hadn't realized something had been on him until then. He didn't stop to question what that something was. He used his worry and fear as a weapon as he burst free from the rubble and stood, his arms going out, his vision clearing slowly. He soaked in the destruction around him. Smoke filled the area and fires burned to his left and right. The air was thick and hard to breathe, but he didn't care. His only concern was Alice.

Where the hell was she?

He'd been holding her to him as guards shot at them and then bam, everything had gone dark. Looking around, it seemed like the whole building had collapsed in his area. With a jerk, he spun to see that an entire cinderblock wall had been what had fallen on him.

Fear ate at him. Alice wouldn't have survived something like that. He should have been more banged up than he was, especially considering that prior to the explosion he'd been riddled with bullet wounds. He didn't want to dwell on what the scientists had done to him. Now wasn't the time. Whatever they'd done had made it so he was able to at least search for his woman.

Mine, he thought, his heart still racing.

And she was missing.

Twisting more, he sniffed the air again, forcing himself to filter out everything but her scent. He caught it then, faint but there. The smell of strawberries and mint.

Alice!

The wolf continued to beat at him, and he let it peek through slightly, enhancing his senses even more. He dropped to where he'd just been and saw her then, lying there, not moving. He grabbed for her as gently as he could with his state of mind. The wolf reacted, clawing at his gut, demanding he do something because she wasn't breathing. It wanted him to do the unthinkable and claim her. For a moment, he feared his wolf would win and he'd do just that.

"Alice!" he shouted, lifting her and cradling her against his frame. He held her with one arm and grabbed for her face with the other. He cupped her mouth and was about to do a bastardized form of CPR when she gasped and laced her fingers through his hair, drawing him closer to her as her lips collided with his. Her tongue darted past his tongue and he growled, low and deep as need slammed through him.

Try as he might to control himself, he couldn't. He'd spent too long being pumped endlessly with drugs that made him desire sex, and his wolf was too close to the surface. Need poured off Alice and Brad couldn't deny her, even if he'd wanted to, which he did not. His tongue moved around hers in expert fashion as if the two had years of practice together rather than mere seconds.

It felt as if someone had tied a rope around his waist, connecting him to Alice. He'd had a similar sensation when, after his last beating with silver-coated chains, he'd had fleeting images of a pale redhead in need. His jaw sagged in disbelief as he put it all together, who the woman from his vision was—Alice.

He knew he should back away and make sure she was safe and sound, but he couldn't seem to gather control or stop kissing her. He took their kiss to another level, his tongue delving deeper. He yanked harder on her, trying to kiss his way through her. The feeling of being tied to her increased to the point he actually thought he might have managed to fuse to her.

His cock responded to the idea, liking it very much. So much that it seemed to have a mind of its own. He couldn't recall a time he'd ever been this hard, this desperate to have sex. He didn't care about anything other than her and being one with her.

Her eyes snapped open and she pushed on his chest, breaking their kiss, a look of sheer terror on her face. The sight ripped at his gut. He didn't want her afraid of him.

"Alice," he said softly. "I'm sorry. You kissed me, and well, I couldn't stop myself from kissing you back."

She kept her hand on his chest and began to caress it. "Did I hurt you?"

His brows met. Was she serious? Sure, she'd hurt him if she thought giving him a raging hard-on equaled pain. In all honesty, it sort of did. He had to reach down and adjust himself in an attempt to alleviate some of the pressure in his cock.

"No, baby," he said softly. "You didn't hurt me. Whatever you did actually made me feel better."

"It did?" she asked, confusion coating her beautiful face.

Baby?

Did I just baby *her?*

She blinked several times and then

coughed. Blood shot out of her mouth and trickled down her chin and neck. The false sense of relief he'd gained from her speaking to him vanished and he realized just how hurt she was. She'd clearly sustained internal injuries during the explosion.

Her eyes widened and she gripped his hand. He bent and kissed her forehead gently. "I'll get you to help."

She shook her head and tugged on him, forcing him to lean. "Succubus."

He'd heard Ezra refer to her as such already. Why was she bothering to tell him again? Did she not think he knew better than to take her to a human hospital? He'd reach out to his contacts underground as soon as he knew it was safe and find her medical help that catered to supernaturals. "I know, baby."

Cringing, he realized he'd given her the same pet name once more.

She shook her head, her eyes wide. She winced and additional blood came from her mouth. "Need sex energy."

It took Brad a moment to wrap his mind around what she was telling him. When it hit him, he lifted his brows. "Where do I find that?"

The look Alice gave him was a cross between annoyance and amusement. She ran her hand over his cheek in a sweeping motion, as if they were lovers. "*You*. Need you."

She needed him?

The knowledge rocked him to his very core.

She coughed and then cried out before her eyes rolled into the back of her head. She passed out in his arms and he lifted her carefully. He'd get her to safety and he'd figure out a way to see to her needs, though he was pretty sure she'd been delirious when she'd suggested she needed him.

He held her to him closely as he made his way through the rubble in the direction he could only hope was out. With as disoriented as he was he half-feared he'd walk straight into the enemy's hands. The further he went, the more he got his wits about him. When he exited out into open air and found himself standing in what used to be a parking lot, the building he'd come from engulfed in flames, he backed up more, holding Alice protectively. Everything in him wanted to run with her, far and fast, but he couldn't risk hurting her more.

He'd get her somewhere safe and he'd see to her medical needs as best he could. And if he absolutely had to, he'd reach out to some of his old SEAL buddies. He had to be careful. Trusting others had landed him where he was —a prisoner. He wouldn't jeopardize Alice's safety. He spotted a vintage muscle car off a ways in the parking area. There was no doubt in his mind the car belonged to a guard. Men like them went for muscle cars.

He went straight for the vehicle. If he knew the guards like he suspected he did, the car would have a stash of weapons and cash in it in the event a quick getaway was needed. With great care he set Alice on the hard ground and then proceeded to break into the car. Once he'd gained access he placed Alice in the passenger seat. He then rushed around, assumed the driver's seat and proceeded to hotwire the vehicle. The skill was one he'd picked up during his squandered youth, but one he was happy to have.

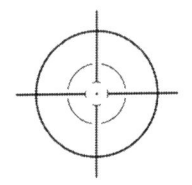

Chapter Nine

Brad drove as fast as he could, and for as long as he dared with the condition Alice was in before he pulled down a one-lane road and found a secluded spot to park off to the side. They were far enough from the highway that no one would think to look for them there. He needed to check on her.

She hadn't moved since he'd put her in the car, and he'd spent the last hour listening to her breathing as he drove, scared beyond words that she'd give up the fight and die. That just wasn't an option. He needed her.

He stilled, trying to understand where the feelings had come from. Had he developed them because he'd been held so long and she represented something to him—freedom maybe? Or was it something more, something deeper? Whatever it was, he wanted her safe.

"Alice? Baby?" He touched her cheek with the back of his knuckles. When she didn't respond his chest tightened. Had he done the right thing by taking her from the holding facility? They were bastards, but they would have seen to her medical attention if for no other reason than to ensure they'd get top dollar for her or possibly be able to breed her. Had he put her life in more jeopardy by removing her from a location that had doctors trained for supernatural care?

His hand shook as he touched her face gently once more. "Alice."

Her eyes flickered open, and she sucked in what sounded like a painful breath. "B-Brad?"

"Shh, baby, we're safe. We're out of the place, but you're hurt. Bad."

Her hand moved over his. "Need to feed."

He tensed. Did he trust himself enough to give her what her body required? When his mind screamed "hell no" he knew the answer, but that didn't change the fact Alice was a succubus and from what he was quickly beginning to recognize, she needed sex to help her heal.

Man up, Durant, he thought. *She needs you to pull your shit together.*

"Yes," Alice said, a lazy smile moving over her beautiful face. "She does."

He stared at her for a moment before realizing she'd picked up on his thoughts. "You can read me?"

"Couldn't before," she whispered, wincing and shifting slightly in the seat. "I can now after we kissed. Weird. Your thoughts aren't like others."

He lifted a brow. What the hell did that mean? Had the doctors broken him mentally too, like they'd broken his wolf?

She touched his hand. "They don't fill my

head and make a lot of noise. They feel good. Right."

He touched her lower lip, wanting to kiss her again. "Tell me how to help you. I know you need sex. What can I do to help you with that?"

The look she gave him was priceless. "I doubt I need to explain to you what to do with a woman, or do I?"

His cheeks flamed nearly as red as her hair. "No. Believe it or not, baby, I was once considered a ladies' man."

It was her turn to cock a brow in disbelief. "Sure."

Brad smiled, and it felt good to have a happy moment after so many miserable ones over the past months. His happiness was short-lived as Alice coughed and more blood trickled down her chin.

Brad reacted, jumping out of his side of the vehicle and racing around to hers. He opened her door, reached in, lifted her out, and then moved her instinctively to the hood of the car. He set her on it gently. "Alice, tell me what to do."

She grabbed his face and tugged, drawing his mouth close to hers. Their lips met, and Brad shut off everything but the taste and feel of the woman in his arms. Her blood coated his tongue, enticing his shifter side in ways that both worried and excited him. His wolf beat at him from the inside, wanting him to be more aggressive, to take her and pound into her until he was fully spent and she was fully claimed. The thought should have sobered him. It didn't. It excited him, and that worried him.

She wrapped her legs around him and yanked his body over hers. Brad went willingly, grinding his lower half against hers as their kiss took hold. He felt it then, her magik again, moving up and around him. His dick responded in kind, lengthening, readying itself for whatever she wanted and needed. The drugs the guards had been putting in his food were still in his system, and that worried him. He was already on edge, his wolf bigger and more aggressive than it ever had been. He didn't want to harm Alice.

"Alice," he said, breaking the kiss for the briefest of moments. "I'm so fucking scared of hurting you."

She bit his lower lip hard enough to draw blood from him and let out a sultry laugh. "Pain can be fun, Bradley."

He slammed his hands on the hood of the car and ravished her mouth, going at her hard and heavy, his hips moving as if he was making love to her, rather than merely grinding against her. It didn't matter. It all felt so good, he didn't care. Her magik made him feel whole again, and he could sense the burning need running through her for more of what they were doing.

She ran her hands over his bare chest and then reached up and cupped his face. It was Alice who broke the kiss, looking him over closely, turning his head left and then right. "Am *I* hurting you?"

"No, baby. I told you before, whatever you do makes me feel more alive than I've ever felt."

She panted. "Tell me if I start to hurt you, please."

"I will."

She put her lips to his, and he caught her chin, holding her back from kissing him full on once more. He eased his tongue out and over her lower lip slowly and then licked the dried blood from her chin. The act was so erotic to his shifter side that Brad thought he might come where he stood. Alice wiggled beneath him, pushing her mound against his distended flesh. He reacted, moving in a way that left him drawing tiny moans of pleasure from her. He kept going, kept dry fucking her on the hood of the car he'd stolen.

Alice grabbed hold of his arms and cried out, her magik hitting him harder, giving him more energy. Before he could register what was happening his seed shot free of him, filling the scrub bottoms he was wearing. Alice's blue eyes filled with black for a second and then returned to normal as a lazy smile spread across her face.

"Thank you," she said, drifting off in his arms.

Her breathing was no longer labored, and he couldn't sense her pain anymore. Manly pride welled in him and he lifted her, placing her back in the passenger seat. He buckled her in once more and then stood and looked around the area. There was a grazing cow in a pasture not far from them, chewing on grass and giving him a look that said she knew what they'd been up to.

Brad smiled wide and drew in a deep breath, enjoying the smell of freedom, even if it came with the added aroma of cow manure. Glancing down at himself, he took note of the wet spot all over the front of his bottoms. He grunted and then went to the trunk of the car to look around. The guards were crafty bastards. They'd want a quick exit strategy and would need to be able to go on the run for extended periods with ease.

He'd been around the block enough to spot hidden compartments. By the time he was done taking inventory of what was in the trunk and several other compartments he found in the backseat area, they had a good stockpile of weapons and ammunition, enough cash to start new lives and a decent amount of men's clothing and shoes. There wasn't anything for a woman. As much as Brad hated the guards, they were predictable and clearly paid well for their nefarious acts.

Without hesitation, he removed the bottoms he'd been wearing and tossed them aside. The damn cow made a noise, reminding him he was being watched. He dressed in a pair of jeans that fit his frame now, but wouldn't have fit his frame prior to being taken. Brad, while still toned and fit, wasn't as bulky as he had been. His exercise had been limited to what he could do in a cell, but he'd been sure to take every opportunity he could to stay in tiptop shape. He slipped on a T-shirt and a pair of work boots that would do for now.

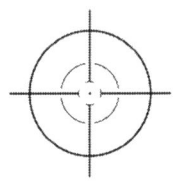

Chapter Ten

Brad finished refueling the car and put the pump back in place before looking again, making sure they weren't being followed and hadn't been found. He'd had to leave Alice sleeping in the car long enough to go into a store and get some personal items for them and clothing for her. He'd grabbed some fresh fruit and bottled water as well, unsure if she'd be hungry when she woke. He needed to find a safe place for them to spend the night. Ezra's safe house was an option, but Brad didn't want to take it just yet. Not until he knew for sure Ezra could be trusted. He wanted to believe the man could, but he'd been fooled before, and he wouldn't risk Alice.

They were hours from the holding facility, but that didn't take from Brad's paranoia. While he didn't want to go back and be under the thumb of madmen, the idea of allowing them to get their hands on Alice again did something to him that he couldn't explain. He'd rather be locked away for the remainder of his immortally long life than permit harm to come to her again.

Deep down, he knew she was a liability. That he should reach out to his old network for her, for help, and then walk away, but he couldn't do it. He couldn't fathom the idea of simply stepping out of her life.

You barely know her.

As he took his spot behind the steering wheel, his gaze returned to Alice. She was resting at an angle that appeared uncomfortable. He reached back in a bag on the seat behind him, withdrew a shirt and rolled it before placing it gently under her head. She moaned lightly, her lips so close to his face that he could have kissed her.

It took all of him not to.

"Keep sleeping, baby," he said in a hushed tone, wanting her to get as much sleep as possible. It would help her heal fully. At least he hoped it would.

He got back on the road, wanting more distance between them and the facility they'd been held at. He ate a banana as he drove, but found he was only able to take a few bites. His stomach wasn't used to whole foods. As the sun set, Brad pulled to the side of the highway, thankful they'd been the only car on the isolated stretch for nearly an hour. He had to stretch his legs, and he wasn't entirely sure the little portion of the fruit he ate was going to remain down.

He put the car in park and was about to open the driver's side door when Alice stirred once more, hissing, her eyes snapping open. He expected her to scream, to fight, to be afraid and unsure of where she was or who she was with. She met his gaze and reached for him as the vehicle filled with the smell of her desire. Her eyes swirled with liquid black.

Brad gasped, understanding it was Alice's succubus. That, like in the hall after the explosion, she needed to feed it. And if her eyes were swirling to black he suspected she was pretty far gone on the control side of things. A pang of guilt hit him. She'd said she needed him to feed her hunger before, but he'd been reluctant to do so.

She ripped at the seatbelt holding her in place. Brad reached around her and undid it before she either hurt herself or managed to tear it to shreds. She moved up and over the center console in the blink of an eye. She straddled his waist, and he thumped his head backwards, wanting to be a gentleman and avoid taking her while she was under the influence of her succubus, but his wolf didn't really give a shit. It wanted her and didn't care what was driving her.

He did his best to hold her, but she was damn strong in this state. Brad's wolf rose to the challenge, surging forward, stealing his control. She ran her hands into his hair, her lips finding his. The second her tongue found its way to his, he felt invigorated. His stomach stopped protesting the small bit of food he'd managed. Alice ground her hips on his lap, his cock hardening at once, wanting free from the jeans he'd put on. She undid his pants and shoved her hand down, finding him hard and ready for her.

She stopped the kiss and moved back, freeing his cock from the jeans. It twitched in her hand, and she grinned a grin so sexy that Brad reached out and touched her lips. He stared up at her, taking in all of her beauty. Tiny freckles were sprinkled over her nose and upper cheeks. He wanted to kiss every single one of them. She was stunning and there was something so familiar about her.

Her lips found his once more. She kept her hand on his cock and began stroking it with rapid motions, her lips remaining locked against his. Brad stiffened and tried to lift her, wanting to give her pleasure too. Alice pushed hard on him with her free hand, keeping him pinned in place with more than just sheer strength. He smelled something different on her. Something more.

He opened his eyes, his tongue wrapped around hers. Magik. He smelled magik and it was coming from Alice, keeping him pinned in place. His wolf, which had been so eager to get a shot at sex with Alice, didn't take kindly to having her in charge. It was alpha, and it wasn't about to allow him roll over and let a woman take control.

It struggled, wanting to be freed, but he knew better. It was unpredictable, and he'd never willingly allow it out around Alice. He wouldn't risk her.

His hand found its way to her long red

hair and she tore her mouth from his. Hunger reflected back at him and he knew he was nearly as out of control as she was.

"Hurts," she whispered, flecks of blue mixing in the with the black in her eyes.

"Come back to me, baby," said Brad, running his thumb over her cheek. "I want you, but not like this. I won't take you when something else is controlling your actions."

He wasn't so sure he believed his own words. He'd managed to hold out all that time against everything the doctors did to him only to nearly lose it all in the front seat of a car with some chick he'd just met.

She's more than just some chick, he thought, caressing her cheek more.

Moisture coated Alice's eyes, and she trembled on his lap. "I'm here," she whispered. "I'm in here."

He cupped her face, wanting to kiss her but restraining. "Alice?"

She managed a slight nod. "She's letting me up."

"She?" he asked, not following.

"H-Harlot," she pressed between clenched teeth.

It took Brad a bit to get her meaning, and when he did, he understood. Her succubus. Alice felt as removed from it as he did with his wolf anymore. And right now that driving force in her was permitting Alice, the woman, to have some semblance of control.

"Tell me what to do," Brad said, continuing to hold her face gently. "I can feel your need, your hunger, and it's beating at my willpower. I'll take you wherever you want to go. Who can help you heal, baby? Tell me and I'll make it happen. I'll do anything for you."

The words caused him to take pause.

Alice began stroking his cock once more, additional blue showing through the black in her eyes. She leaned in. "You. I pick you. No one else. *She* wants it to be you too. Only you."

He had to turn his face from her, his teeth threatening to lengthen as he and the wolf had a moment of celebration at her words. She wanted him. As much as he wanted to tear the thin bits of scrubs from her, he didn't trust his control. And he certainly didn't trust his fucking wolf.

"I can't," he managed, but just barely as she increased her hand movements on his shaft.

"Please."

A piece of him broke as he heard the small, helpless plea come from her. He nodded, unable to speak for fear he'd let the wolf free. She put her face close to his once more and it was Brad who started the kiss but Alice who then took the lead. Again his wolf wanted to protest the idea of someone else being in charge. It wanted him to put her in the backseat of the car, tear every strip of clothing from her and then ram deep inside her. It wanted to claim every inch of the pale beauty seated on his lap. But Brad wasn't sure the wolf would stop there. Whatever had been done to him left the wolf almost feral and he didn't want to think harder on what it might do to Alice should he let it out.

She kept jerking him off as she rubbed herself against him. Having her touching him in such a way and kissing him was all too much. Between it and his wolf wanting to show everyone who was in charge, Brad found himself doing the unthinkable—surrendering completely.

He was well and thoroughly beaten. She'd done what the guards couldn't. She'd broken him, but the price was one he was willing to pay. She needed this. She needed to be in control and to take whatever it was she wanted from him. Brad stopped trying to lift her off him and yanked on her, allowing her to lead their kiss fully.

At the same moment, his balls tightened,

and he knew he wouldn't be able to hold off his orgasm any longer. More importantly, he didn't want to. The wolf felt the pending climax as well and yanked back, stopping its attempts at freedom. He nearly laughed. Even his wolf was man enough to admit it wanted to come by the redhead's hands.

Alice's magik wrapped around Brad's cock at the same time that she bit down on his tongue, drawing blood. Coppery fluid filled his mouth, and Alice shocked him by drinking it down, her hand strokes increasing. Unable to stop himself, Brad exploded all over her hand, his stomach and part of hers. His teeth began to lengthen and the strongest deep-set need to bite the woman on him, hit him hard. His brief surrender ended, and he stiffened, trying to gain control of the situation.

Alice broke their kiss, her eyes filled with only the smallest flecks of black now. A sexy, satisfied smile tugged at her lush lips as she ran her hand up and down his cock, smearing his seed all over him. She brought her hand to her lips and licked it clean, making him want to be in her.

He groaned. "Off."

She remained in place.

"Alice, please. I can't control the wolf anymore," he pleaded.

She gasped and then blinked, the blue totally gone from her gaze this time. "I won't fight the claim. It's destined and she'll come around to the idea."

He closed his eyes tight. Those words should have meant everything to him. All they did was terrify him. It was then he realized why his control was so poor around her.

She can't be my mate. The odds of that are…

She leaned against him. "I have to go back for Mae."

With a heavy heart, Brad spoke, "Alice, baby, there is nothing left to go back to. The explosion took out the building."

"No," she whispered, tensing against him.

He kissed her gently, sharing in her pain at the loss of Mae. "Yes."

Alice's eyelids fluttered a half-second before she passed out face first against his shoulder. He caught her to him, the sticky aftermath of his pleasure all over the front of both of them. He wrapped his arms around Alice's slight frame and gave a gentle squeeze, sensing the extreme exhaustion on her. He silently admitted he was tired as well. He didn't want to let her go, but knew they needed to get back on the road. He'd find a spot for them to hunker down for the night and then he'd figure out what the hell it was he was going to do from there.

He returned her to her seat, buckled her in with great care and then did his best to wipe the aftermath of everything from her and himself. Cleaned as best as he could be, Brad started the car and pulled back onto the road, going in the direction his gut said to go. The heavy pull of it all began to wear on him and he drove until he could no longer keep his eyes open. A small roadside motel was just up ahead. It was a welcome sight even though it was hardly five stars. The place would be lucky if it received one star.

Beggars can't be choosers.

He was fairly sure Alice wouldn't approve of the joint. Something about her said she was used to the finer things in life, and this place was far from that.

Very far.

Most of the letters on the light-up sign were burned out, leaving the sign making little sense. A snort broke free of him. The cell he'd just come from was probably cleaner than the rooms at the motel. In the end, it didn't matter. They were free and that was the focus. Nothing more.

Brad checked on Alice once again before grabbing some cash and heading into the front office. With the time of the night and absence of any cars in the parking lot, he assumed he'd walk in and find one person behind the counter and no one else. He was wrong.

He did a double take as he found a rather tall, skinny, pale man who was dressed as a pirate standing in the corner of what he supposed was a lobby of sorts. In reality it was just a decent-sized room with carpet that looked to have been installed prior to his birth and an air conditioning unit in the wall that was on the fritz. The pirate guy turned in several slow circles, never once making eye contact with anyone yet Brad got the feeling the man was seeing everything.

His time in the SEALs had left him meeting a lot of interesting and colorful people. He couldn't recall a time he'd met someone dressed as a pirate when it wasn't even close to Halloween. Maybe the guy was into role-playing fetishes. Who knew?

Whatever works for the guy, he thought as he glanced at the other man in the lobby. This one was sitting, holding a magazine that was from the mid-nineties, not to mention upside down. The man was dressed like he'd just walked out of the seventies. He had on a pair of polyester, bell-bottom pants, a shirt with an oversized collar and a brown leather jacket. The fedora on his head of wiry, graying hair really sealed the deal. The man's gut was bigger than the shirt allowed room for and Brad watched, holding in a laugh, as a button popped free.

The short, pudgy man glanced up at the taller guy dressed like a pirate. "Stop. I know you told me it didn't fit. I don't want to hear you nag me anymore, Gus."

Brad glanced at the woman behind the counter to see if she was watching the interplay between two men who were clearly not right in the head. The pirate hadn't said a word yet the little guy continued to talk to him as if they were having an argument.

The woman behind the counter was engrossed in a reality TV show playing on a small television set up in the room. She was puffing on a cigarette. Brad wasn't sure how the ashes from it remained intact, but they did. The woman cleared her throat and then glanced at him briefly. "Want a room?"

"Yes, please," he said, glancing at the men to his right once more.

The wiry-haired guy pretended to be engrossed in his upside-down magazine while the pirate kept turning in a circle.

"One night or one hour?" asked the woman, looking past him at his car parked out front.

Brad stiffened at the suggestion Alice was a prostitute and he was a client. He pulled out a wad of cash and realized that he fit the bill nicely. No wonder the woman thought that of him. He was driving an expensive sports car, had a hot girl in the passenger seat and was trying to rent a room at a hole-in-the ground motel.

"The night," he said, paying the woman

and slipping her extra money. He leaned in and rattled off additional requests for a room, making sure it was one he could secure easier than others. When the woman nodded and handed him a key, he slipped her another twenty. "Can you make sure if anyone asks..."

She looked back at her TV show. "You were never here."

It was plain to see she dealt with a lot of questionable characters. That was probably why she didn't seem to pay any mind to the two crazy guys in her lobby who were still having a one-sided argument.

Brad paused before leaving the office. "You all right?"

The wiry-haired guy stood up fast and nodded. "Right as rain. Aren't we, Gus?"

The pirate didn't reply, but he did stop turning in a circle.

"Gus says hi," the wiry-haired one added.

Brad looked the pirate up and down

slowly. "Uh, hi, Gus. Pleasure to meet you."

The wiry-haired one grinned and then quickly schooled his face. "Don't mind us. We're just two inconspicuous guys. That's right. Nothing to see here. We're not on a secret mission or anything. Just two badass dudes here enjoying an evening out."

The man was seriously insane.

"Okay then. Have a nice night," said Brad, walking out slowly, wondering if any mental wards had recent breakouts.

He made it back to the car, got in and pulled around to the side with the room he'd rented. As he prepared to get Alice, he noticed the men from the lobby standing on the corner of the hotel, the wiry-haired one looking in their direction. While Brad was sure they were nuts, they probably thought he was some kind of a serial killer with the way he was lifting an unconscious woman and carrying her into a seedy motel.

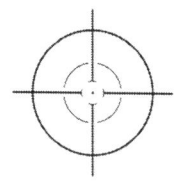

Chapter Eleven

Alice continued to stare at the bare, lush backside of the incredible male specimen in the bed next to her. The man was out cold and hadn't moved a muscle since she'd awoken to find herself in bed with him. This was hardly her first time waking up next to a hot, naked guy, but this was the first time that she didn't want to run away.

No, she wanted to touch this man. She wanted to know *every* inch of him.

She kept the sheet pulled up and against her even though she was wearing a T-shirt she didn't remember putting on. That was no surprise. She often woke fully naked or wearing someone else's clothing. A side effect of her inner harlot coming out to play. The fraternity party must have been really fun because she couldn't remember much beyond heading out of her dorm to attend it.

Reaching out, she touched the man's back lightly. His skin was feverous, and concern lanced her. Confused as to why she'd care about some random dude she picked up at a party, Alice eased even closer to him. Normally, this would have been when she snuck away, made her exit and didn't look back. The very idea of walking away from this man sickened her.

As she touched his skin, she noticed the faintest hints of scars crisscrossing his otherwise perfect form. Upon closer inspection she realized that very little of him was without the scarring. She traced the lines of one of the shiny lines and felt her anger growing. Whoever hurt him would pay. She'd see to it. She kept coming back to the scarring around his shoulder and arm. When she'd first been taken she'd had bruises that seemed to have come out of nowhere, if you believed the eyewitness at the time, that matched where the man's scars were.

Strange.

Very strange indeed.

Uncharacteristically, she leaned and kissed his shoulder tenderly. As her lips made contact with his hot skin, emotions welled for him, only serving to confuse her more. She didn't form emotional attachments with men ever. What the hell had happened at that party to make her do so now?

She closed her eyes briefly, and concentrated on the night before. As she did, the events of the past two weeks became clear, coming back to her in one fast wave. The man next to her wasn't some random guy she picked up at a frat party. It was Brad. The man who had carried her to freedom over his shoulder through fire, and who had taken bullets in an attempt to protect her.

She gasped as she thought about waking up in a car, her succubus ravenous. She'd used Brad to sate her needs more than once.

No, she thought. *I tried to use him fully, but he didn't let me. He didn't want to take me when I wasn't in control.*

Additional emotions filled her for the man. She'd known so many in her life who would have tried to gain control of the situation, who would have simply done whatever to her and walked away. Not Brad.

As she stared harder at the back of his sleeping form, she smiled softly as she realized his hair was shorter now. Still below his shoulders, but not the length she'd first seen on him. Alice eased up and glanced over him, smiling more when she saw that he'd trimmed his beard as well. No longer did he look unkempt. Far from it. The man looked like a male model passed out next to her.

It was hard to keep her sexual need from stirring. She didn't want it to come out and play just yet. She wanted to simply look her fill of Brad and enjoy the moment. Her damn succubus had other things in mind. While she'd used Brad to take the edge off her hunger, she'd not fully fed her inner harlot in nearly a month. The fraternity party was going to be where she fed her fill, but that hadn't gone as planned. After being held captive for so long and then injured, she'd more than used up any sexual energy reserves she'd banked. She needed to feed that side of herself fully and soon.

Brad had already done so much for her. He'd gotten her out of the prison she'd been in, and he'd helped her heal without taking advantage of the situation. She couldn't ask more of him, but the idea of going elsewhere for sex or sexual energy didn't sit well with her.

She wanted him. So did the succubus and they rarely agreed on anything.

"No," she said softly. "He needs rest."

Taking a deep breath, she sat up and stared around the dimly lit room, wondering what time warp she'd gotten stuck in. From the overabundance of paneling and seventies décor, she hazarded a guess they were in a roadside motel. The shag carpeting was matted in the high traffic areas and the bedspread, crumpled on the floor, was straight out of the seventies. So was the rest of the place.

Brad hadn't budged, and she highly doubted he was the type of guy who let someone close to him while he was asleep, especially after the ordeal he'd gone through. Yet, he was letting her close, letting her touch him without incident. He was beyond exhausted. Guilt hit her hard. She'd taken from him when he'd had nothing to offer. When he'd been battered and broken too. Probably more so than her.

Alice eased out of the bed and covered him with the sheet. She'd clean up while he rested. He'd earned some sleep. As much as she wanted to phone her father for his help in the matter, her gut told her not to do anything that might draw the attention of the enemy. She didn't fear for herself. She worried for Brad. She knew deep down the man wouldn't survive being held again.

No.

She'd wait to contact her father until she knew for sure they were safe. For now, she'd clean up and then do her best to help take care of Brad for a bit. He'd earned it and more.

Had the bathroom facilities been slightly better she would have probably stayed in the shower forever, wanting the grime of the last week off her. She hurried to clean herself and then exited into the bathroom. There was a small bag from one of those stores that carried just about anything you could think of and stayed open all night. In the bag were clothes in her size and next to it sat a pair of red flip-flops.

Alice of two weeks ago wouldn't have been caught dead dressing in anything other than designer from head to toe. The Alice who had come out of the other side of being held against her will had never seen a sweeter gift in her life. She teared up as she dressed. He'd not only risked his life for her and fed her succubus respectfully, he'd also apparently made a stop to be sure she had clothing, even with as tired and hurt as he'd been.

Her gaze moved to his sleeping form. She wanted to go to him, kiss him tenderly and profess feelings for him that she shouldn't have yet. Feelings that were too strong for a man she'd only just met. She resisted.

Brad still hadn't moved, and she knew he had to be hungry. It was her turn to care for him. Before long, she'd secured some cash from one of the bags on the table and took the keys to the car. She was about to leave when she spotted another small bag. When she opened it, she found several handguns. Her father had taught her to shoot when she was young and had made sure she kept up on the skill. He was a big believer in always being prepared and able to protect yourself.

He'd be disappointed she'd gotten grabbed. She'd known better. She shouldn't have been at that party without a buddy. And she certainly shouldn't have been walking around at night by herself. Then again, Bart shouldn't have been a giant douchebag who kidnapped women, so there was that.

Alice lifted the smallest of the weapons and slid it into the waist of her pants, using her shirt to cover it. She wasn't going to make the same mistake again. If the creeps who had held her and Brad were still looking for them, she'd be ready. And she wouldn't hesitate to shoot one. They would not touch Brad again. Not while she was still breathing.

He's mine, she thought, gasping at the clarity she felt at the statement.

As she stepped out of the motel door, she had to squint, the sun was shining so brightly. It had been some time since she'd felt its warm rays upon her skin, and while she did burn easily and tended to avoid it as much as possible, sunlight was exactly what she needed. She made her way to the car and paused near the hood, her thoughts going back to when Brad had dry-humped her on it. Her body tingled with remembered pleasure.

She ran her fingers over the hood lightly and glanced to the side. She froze. There, near the edge of the motel, was a short man dressed like a pimp, and a tall man next to him dressed as a pirate. Both were staring at her. When she tipped her head, they turned their backs to her at once. They looked as if they were trying hard to appear normal and avoid detection.

They were failing miserably.

"Hello there," she said loudly, making the pirate jolt.

The pimp glanced over his shoulder at her. "Just two guys enjoying an early morning stroll. Nothing to see here, Little Red."

Little Red?

She continued to stare at the men,

something tugging at her gut, telling her they were harmless and could be trusted. The feeling hitting her also made her want to walk up and hug them. She resisted.

The pimp began to wiggle in place doing what could only be described as a preschooler's peepee dance. He looked up at the pirate. "I know you said to go before we left our room, but I didn't have to go then. No. Don't yell at me. You sound like the meanies back at headquarters. If I wanted someone to boss me around, I'd have stayed there."

The pirate hadn't uttered a single word, yet the pimp continued on with his one-sided conversation. "I know they're worried about us. We're fine. We're not children. We can do things. We'll show them. Then they'll *have* to let us have a later bedtime."

"Brad, you sure picked an interesting place to stay," she said more to herself as she laughed and got into the car.

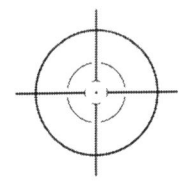

Chapter Twelve

Alice's hands were full with the bags of food from the diner as she opened the door and stepped into the dark room. The minute she closed the door behind her, the hair on the back of her neck rose. Alice froze, fearful that Bart and Nile had found her again.

"I thought you left me," came a deep voice she didn't recognize from the bathroom area.

With the old, heavy curtains drawn and the lights off, Alice couldn't see. She remained in place, fear coursing through her. "W-where is Brad?"

As he stepped out of the bathroom she made out his form. It had been Brad talking to her? But it hadn't sounded like him. The voice had been so much deeper than Brad's already powerful voice.

His wolf!

She stiffened, realizing Brad wasn't in control at the moment. "I went to get food. I was worried about you and wanted to make sure you ate something."

He stepped forward more and came into focus. Fur covered most of his body. His fingers seemed longer, and claws were visible from the tips of them. Brad had already been tall. Now he seemed downright giant to her.

"Brad," she said softly. "You're scaring me."

"I can smell your cunt," he said brazenly.

Alice wasn't shocked by the words so much as his use of them to her. *This isn't Brad*, she thought. *It's his version of an inner harlot. A really big, hairy and deadly version, but a version all the same.*

He reached out and ran the tips of his claws along the wall nearest him. The wallpaper turned into shreds everywhere he touched, floating to the floor in a hypnotic-like motion, and she knew he wasn't even applying pressure. If he could do that to the wall, she didn't want to think on what he could do to a person with those claws. She could only imagine it wouldn't be pretty or hypnotic in the least.

Her mind said drop the food and run, but deep down she knew that would be very bad. That whatever was happening to Brad wouldn't be helped by kicking his prey drive into high gear. If she did, the thrill of the chase, of the hunt, could take control of him. It could cause him to hurt her without meaning to. That was something she certainly didn't want to have happen.

She'd never been more thankful than to have a shifter father. He'd spoken of the blood lust before. Of the crazed state shifter males could enter. He'd said that when it came over men, they weren't themselves, and he said what seemed to always be the trigger was their mates being in danger.

Her brows met. That didn't make any sense. Was Brad's mate in trouble? And why did the thought of him having a significant other bother her so much?

His nostrils flared. "You weren't here when I woke. At first, I thought they took you and then I realized their scents weren't here. Only yours was." He moved closer to her. "You left me."

The need to flee was still great. She held back, taking a deep breath and doing as her father had taught her once long ago. She was going to show no fear to the predator before her. At least that was the plan, if her legs would stop trembling at the sight of him. Even partially shifted he was magnificent. Scary as hell, but gorgeous all the same. Though, her strong love of children's movies and fairytales did make her think instantly of the tale of Little

Red Riding Hood. She very much felt like the main character now that she had her own big bad wolf to contend with. She just hoped hers didn't want to eat her.

"Knock it off, Bradley," she said sternly, hoping she wasn't letting off any signs of fear. "I went to get you food. I wanted you fed. Now shut up and eat this food before I force feed it to you."

He's going to tear my head off.

He blinked and then looked around, seeming to come out of a trance. Lifting his hands, he stared at them and then leapt back. Shaking his head, horror stricken, he spoke, "Oh gods, Alice."

She practically tossed the food onto the table before rushing towards him. She hated seeing the pain in his dark gaze.

He put his clawed hands up, his eyes wide, his body still partially shifted. "Run!"

Alice grabbed for him, mindful of the

claws. "Bradley."

"Run," he ground out, going to his knees. "Can't control the wolf."

Alice went to her knees as well, and did the only thing she could think to do. She grabbed his face and kissed him. As their tongues wound around one another, she felt the fur on his arms fading away, replaced by smooth skin. Smiling against his lips, she kept kissing him. It felt too good to stop.

He broke the kiss and stared at her with wide, fright-filled eyes. "I could have killed you."

"I don't think so," she returned, going for his lips again.

He caught her shoulders. "Are you insane?"

She shrugged. "It's been up for debate for years."

He sighed, a level of tiredness in his voice as he spoke. "Alice, be serious here. If you ever see me in that state again, get as far from me as you can."

Still on her knees, she raked her gaze down his naked form. The man had the best cock. She could still remember what it felt like, even with the succubus in control, holding his velvety smooth shaft in her hands. It took her a minute to realize he was still talking to her. From the sounds of it, he was upset.

"Are you even listening to me, woman?" he demanded.

She shook her head. "No. I was focused on your dick."

His eyes widened. "W-what?"

"Your dick," she repeated, wondering if shifting left him dazed and confused like her succubus sometimes did to her. "It's a great dick, Brad. You should be very proud of it."

He huffed. "Are you serious?"

"Very." She grinned and then bit her lower lip. "I do not joke about cocks."

His expression hardened. "Just how many cocks have you seen?"

She tipped her head. "Not sure. A lot though. And trust me, yours is awesome."

He didn't seem excited by the news. In fact, he looked like he might wolf out again at any moment. "Alice, if you know what's good for you, you won't ever mention seeing other men's dicks again."

She lifted a brow. He did not say what she thought he did, did he? "Know what's good for me?"

He touched her cheek, and she could sense the restraint he was exercising. "Baby, please. I'm holding on by a fucking thread. From the moment I met you I've wanted to be in you. Hearing you talk about my dick is only making that worse. And the wolf is barely caged. It doesn't like knowing you've been with other men. I don't like knowing it either."

"Bradley," she said softly, her anger with him fading fast.

He met her gaze.

"Tell your wolf to either man up and fuck me or shut up and go lie in the corner. I'm not going to roll over and submit. It's not really my style."

He blinked, stunned. "Alice?"

"Yes?" she asked innocently.

"Your succubus isn't riding you," he said as if she wasn't aware of this fact herself.

"I know."

"You want me?" he questioned, appearing at a loss.

Her heart broke for the man. He didn't see his worth. Didn't see how much he meant to her. She put her hand over his which was still on her cheek. "I do."

"Why?"

A tiny giggle erupted from her. "Hell if I know, but I want you more than I've ever wanted anyone in my life."

She waited for his rejection. For him to take his ever-popular high road once more. The man's moral compass pointed true north so much so it was annoying. It took her a second to realize his hand was shaking. She saw it then, him straining with all he had. He was trying to keep control of himself. She knew deep down that he was doing so out of fear of hurting her. She turned her head and drew his thumb into her mouth seductively. She sucked on it, making Brad moan and his cock twitch.

"Alice, baby, please don't do this. I could hurt you. I can't control the wolf," he said, desperation coating his voice.

"Then stop trying to," she replied, yanking her shirt off, leaving her upper half bare to him as they remained on the floor on their knees facing one another.

His gaze snapped to her exposed nipples. He swallowed hard and then closed his eyes tight.

She nearly laughed. "Bradley, enough.

Give in to it. I don't want to fight what is between us, why should you?"

"I could hurt you," he said between clenched teeth. "I don't trust my wolf anymore, Alice, and I sure as hell don't trust him with you."

"Tell me why," she said, touching his cheek. "Explain what you're feeling."

When he looked at her, his eyes showed signs of swirling with colors. An indication he was on edge again. "I want to fuck you until you scream my name, until I spend my seed so deep in you that there is no question you're mine and I want to sink my teeth into your pale, freckled skin as I claim you as mine."

With a gasp, she stood and found herself putting her hand out to him. "Then do it, Bradley."

"What?" he asked, looking up at her.

"Do it."

"Alice, did you hear what I said? I want to

fuck and claim you. Do you understand what that means?"

She put her other hand out to him as well. She did understand what a claim meant in the world of supernaturals. It was something she would have never considered allowing to happen before her capture—before Brad. But everything was on its head now. Nothing felt the same as it once had. There was no way she could return to her normal life if Brad wasn't a part of it. She was linked to the man in a way she suspected had something to do with mates. Her parents had explained the concept to her at a young age, arming her with knowledge of their kind.

"Of course I know what it means. I'd be yours forever and you'd be mine. Don't be boring about this, Bradley. Live a little. We're free now. Why should we put our emotions in a prison just because it's all so new? Unless you don't feel the same for me that I feel for you."

"Oh, I feel the same. Trust me." He took her hand and stood, suddenly towering over her once more. His gaze returned to her exposed nipples and he swallowed hard. "But I'm a broken man now."

"Hardly," she returned.

"You could do much better," he stated.

She gave him a hard look. "I swear you don't see it, do you?"

"See what?"

"How important you are to me." She went to her tiptoes and he bent at the same moment. Their lips connected and Alice reached down, her hands finding his cock. He gasped into her mouth as she stroked him. She wasn't able to do so long because he grabbed her and carried her to the bed. He deposited her on it, making it squeak loudly. The mattress was far from luxurious or up to date. She didn't want to think upon how many people had done the very same thing on the bed that they were doing now. No, her thoughts would remain where they belonged, on Brad.

He grabbed for her bottoms, the eagerness on his face spurring her onwards. The second he had her bottoms free of her, Alice opened her legs to him, needing him to understand how much she wanted and welcomed him.

Brad's gaze snapped to the apex of her thighs. She grinned as he licked his lips and then lowered himself, his head going between her legs at once. He wasted no time as he spread her slit, his tongue finding her heated core. Arching her back, she writhed with pleasure as he eased his tongue in and out of her. He rubbed her clit with his thumb at the same time, adding to the passion building between them.

Alice ran her hands through his hair, liking the length on him. She tugged and held his head in place as her orgasm broke over her.

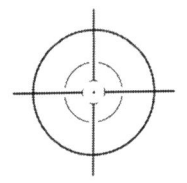

Chapter Thirteen

Brad lapped at Alice's pussy like a depraved man. He'd never tasted anything as divine as her cream. As much as he wanted to spend forever sampling her, his cock was rock hard and ready to burst. He lifted his head from her center and kissed his way up her body slowly, loving the softness she had to her. She was as he liked his woman to be—soft. He had the hard covered enough for them both. He nipped playfully at the underside of her right breast. She giggled and he had to admit he loved the sound of her laughter.

You love more than that, he thought instantly.

He didn't dwell on the feelings he had for her. There was no point. They were what they were and he strongly suspected nature intended for them to be that way. That greater forces than he could ever explain had pulled them together long before they met one another. How else was a headstrong alpha male going to end up mated if it wasn't for Mother Nature's assistance?

Planting a kiss on Alice's throat, he paused, the wolf rushing forward, wanting him to do it—bite her. His breathing increased and he closed his eyes, trying to gather his composure. After several tense seconds, he gained something nearing control and he opened his eyes, staring down at Alice.

She took hold of his cock and guided him to her wet entrance. Brad eased in, gritting his teeth at the tightness surrounding him. He fed himself into her, inch by painfully slow inch. Alice relaxed under him, her fingernails digging into his chest as he progressed. The wolf liked the bite of pain, wanting more than she was currently offering. He went as far as her body would allow and held there for a moment, letting her adjust to his size and girth.

Her jaw went slack as she tilted her head back, giving him her neck. It was such a submissive thing to do that his wolf went wild. It wanted what she was giving him. His teeth felt as if they were going to burst. Brad hooked an arm under one of her legs and lifted it, allowing his cock to settle even deeper into her wetness. When he was hilt deep, he began moving in and out of her, finding a rhythm that left her moaning in his arms.

Her magik peeked out again, coming out to play and join in the fun. Brad wasn't surprised when it wrapped around them and he felt as if another rope was being tied around them. He had come to expect the sensation and welcome it. Feeling it meant he was pleasing Alice and seeing to her needs. He'd always be there for her, always give her whatever her body required.

"Mine," he said, his voice deeper because of the wolf. He bit lightly at the tender skin of her pale neck as he drove himself in and out of her. The taste of her blood coated his tongue.

"Yes. Yours. And you're mine." Alice raked her nails over his upper chest, making blood well. He felt her mouth on the area and her magik increased tenfold, leaving Brad slamming into her, releasing deep, filling her as she hit her climax as well, her magik wound tightly around them.

The wolf roared with victory and then rushed back, allowing Brad full control of the situation now that the deed was done. Now that Alice was his woman.

His wife. He'd bitten her while expending his seed in her and he'd said the word "mine" during it all. For a shifter male, that was it. Brad didn't need the nonexistent manual on being a supernatural to know that. It was inborn.

He licked where he'd bitten her and

watched with great satisfaction as the area healed over at once. He stared down at her, feeling whole and content for the first time in his life. It was as if the void he'd always felt had been waiting to be filled by Alice.

He stayed buried deep in her as he continued to look down at her, locking gazes with her. He grinned. "Thank you."

She scrunched her face. "Wait? You're thanking me for that? Uh, no, it's me who needs to thank you. That was great. I want to do it again."

Chuckling, Brad withdrew slowly from her and then lay on the bed next to her, drawing her frame against his. He kissed her temple. "So there are no misunderstandings later, you know what we just did, right?"

Alice kissed his upper chest. "Bradley, you're being boring again. Stop. I know what we did. I know what it means."

He took a deep breath. "Alice, I get you've got a stubborn streak and I love that about you, but can you possibly do me a favor and avoid feeding your succubus side with other men?"

She propped herself on an elbow and gave him a look that said she was trying not to laugh at him. "Took all of you to say that in the form of a question and not demand it, didn't it?"

With a sheepish grin, he nodded. "Oh yeah. I'm learning that when I let my alpha side out to play, you see it as a challenge and accept it."

She winked. "Keeps things interesting, don't you think?"

He touched her cheek. "Seriously though, as much as it goes against my nature, I will beg."

"Bradley, my inner harlot only wants you for good. So do I," she said, leaning and kissing his lips affectionately, setting his mind at ease. She ran her hand over his torso and then over his cock, working it to a state of hardness quickly. "Though, I might be too much for you."

He laughed as he yanked her up and onto him. "I don't doubt that for a minute. You're a handful, but I think I'm up to the task."

"Good," she said, sliding down onto his cock. "Because I'm only just getting started."

She moved on him in a way that left her tits bouncing before his face. He reached up and cupped them, loving the feel of her on him. The more she moved on him, the more he realized something deep down.

I'm already totally in love with her.

She bent, her lips nearing his. "I know. And ditto."

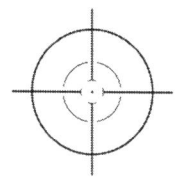

Chapter Fourteen

Brad laughed as he left Alice in the car with the radio going as he stepped out to head into the rest stop. She was busy mouthing the words to a song he remembered being popular some fifteen years or so ago. She'd been full of energy from the moment they'd woken. They'd spent three days in the seedy little roadside motel, only venturing out to the diner when they needed food before they'd moved on to the safe house Ezra had told him about. There had been no sign of Ezra there and Brad knew what that meant.

Something bad had happened to Ezra. He'd not said as much to Alice, but he got the sense she suspected the same thing. Her worry for Mae had increased, as had her desire to check in with her parents. Brad had held her off for as long as he could. They'd been in hiding for over a week. They'd spent the entire time exploring one another fully. He'd spent himself in her in every way possible and still wanted to do it again. He'd never tire of her.

The time had come to move forward and see if the life she'd known was safe to return to or if they'd be on the run for good. Brad didn't give a shit about his life prior. Though, he did want to find out what happened to Vic and he wanted to try to reach out to Kim to make sure she was well. First, he'd see to his mate's needs.

Alice rolled down the window and leaned out a bit, letting her blue gaze rake over him. "Hey, stud muffin, can you grab me a coffee while you're in there?"

"Stud muffin?" Brad groaned at her new pet name for him. He hoped it wouldn't stick.

"I'm not sure you need caffeine. You're hyper enough as it is."

"Because you're keeping my harlot good and fed. I've never felt so alive." Alice laughed, gifting him a smile that tugged at his chest. She winked and they both knew he'd be getting her a coffee. It didn't matter how hyper she was. He'd give in. He knew and so did she.

My wife has me wrapped around her little finger.

Shaking his head and chuckling, Brad headed into the rest stop. He made Alice a cup of coffee, paid and headed back to the parking lot. He stepped out, coffee cup in hand and was confused. The car had been parked not far from the entrance when he'd gone in. Had Alice moved it? Glancing over the nearly empty parking lot, his breathing increased. The morning after their escape, when he'd come to and found her missing, he'd stupidly assumed she'd run out on him. He'd not acknowledged the bond between them and had nearly let his wolf chase her away when she'd returned to him with food. Now that they'd been a couple for several days, he knew better. Knew she wasn't going to up and leave him high and dry.

He also knew Alice was smart enough about his shifter side that she wouldn't try to scare him for no reason. She wouldn't risk him wolfing out in public or at all. No. She'd not moved the car for fun.

He stared around more as dusk settled in fully. His senses picked up, increasing as he took in the sights and sounds around him. It was quiet. Too quiet. While the rest stop hadn't been packed, it had been filled somewhat upon their arrival. It was nearly empty now. Something was wrong. He felt it then, the telltale feeling of being watched—of being stalked by a predator. Not just any bad guy either. He knew this one well.

The smell of cigarettes and indigestion hit him hard, bringing with it flashes of Albin. The fucking guard from Brad's first facility had found him. Fear for Alice's safety nearly caused Brad to do something stupid and tip Albin off that he knew he was close.

"Alice, baby, this isn't funny," he said, pretending nothing was amiss.

When he knew Albin was in striking distance, Brad spun and threw the hot cup of coffee in the man's face. Screaming, Albin grabbed his eyes and staggered backwards. Brad advanced on him and ripped him up by his shirt front. The man's feet dangled off the ground and Brad had to be mindful not to snap the bastard. He needed to know where Alice was before he killed him.

"Where is my woman?" demanded Brad, his wolf pounding at him, wanting released.

Albin snarled at him. "We've got your bitch. Kill me and you'll never find her."

With a sniff of the air, Brad's lip curled. "Funny, I smell at least six more of you fucks. I'm pretty sure if I kill enough of you the last guy left standing will tell me what I want to know."

Albin paled.

Brad lifted him higher off the ground, his wolf there giving him additional strength. Their mate was not to be harmed. They would kill anyone and anything that threatened her.

He was on the verge of ripping out Albin's throat when he heard the muffled sound of Alice's screams. Brad's attention was pulled to the right. There, in the center of the parking lot, was Alice. Two men had her and one had his grubby hand over Alice's mouth. Her blue eyes were wide with fright. They widened more a second before electricity shot through Brad's side.

Hissing, he dropped Albin and doubled over, the pain nearly taking him down fully. As he raised his head he found Albin there with a handheld electric prod, a sick smile on the man's face as he rammed the end of the device into Brad. Jerking, Brad was powerless to stop the effects as they took him to the ground.

Albin leaned over him. "Had them amp up the voltage for animals like you, Durant."

"Bradley!" screamed Alice before she cried out, "Let go of me!"

Albin sneered more, glancing in Alice's direction. "Got yourself a hottie there. Bet she'll feel fucking awesome under me tonight."

Brad did something he'd never dared do in his life—he totally and completely surrendered to his wolf. He actively sought out his wolf, yanking it up from within, demanding it come and do what it wanted to the bastard. He'd risk himself and being locked in wolf form for eternity if it meant Alice was safe. The wolf wasted no time. It surged up and Brad assumed it would take full control and force him to do a complete shift. It didn't. It shifted enough of his body to overcome the effects of the prod and to make Brad good and lethal.

Confusion knit Albin's brow and he rammed the prod into Brad once more. With the wolf and adrenaline riding him high, Brad didn't even respond to the jolt this time. He slashed out with his clawed hand, his nails raking through the tender flesh in Albin's wrist. The prod and the asshole's hand fell to the ground with a sick thud. Satisfaction filled Brad and his wolf as Albin's scream filled the area.

Brad spun and extended his hand once more, this time going for Albin's throat. The guard would never hurt or threaten anyone again. His days had come to an end. Turning, Brad set his sights on the men holding Alice.

Four other men came moving in, all armed, all walking in formation as they came at him from the left side of the parking area. With the wolf in control, it took Brad a moment to realize what he was seeing as a large black van came speeding in at the guards with weapons. The van never slowed as it struck the men, sending two into the air and leaving two others pinned under the front of it.

Brad wasted no time. He used the

distraction to charge in Alice's direction. He was almost to her when she twisted and slammed her fist down and back, hitting one of the men in the groin with enough force that Brad heard it. The man doubled over and screamed. Brad reached Alice just as the other guard near her made a move to use his weapon.

Alice shook her head and then pushed her hands up, hitting the man's arm, making his shot go wide and miss Brad just as Brad grabbed for the man's neck. With a twist, the threat was eliminated.

His woman grabbed for him, seemingly unconcerned with the fact he was partially shifted. She clung to him, shaking and hugging him tight.

"They said they had you," she confessed. "I thought you were dead."

"No," he said, shocked by the wolf's quick draw back. It allowed Brad to take full human form again and seemed quite content with itself. Brad wrapped his arms around Alice and kissed the top of her head. "I'm fine, baby."

She patted his chest and then tensed. "Um, is it me or did a pimp and a pirate just come to our aide?"

"Huh?" Brad turned to find the two men from the motel lobby exiting the black van. The wiry-haired guy came from the driver's side and grinned, showing off his crooked teeth.

"How ya doing?" he asked. "Gus here was worried we wouldn't make it in time to help save you, but I told him we'd be fine."

Confused, Brad shook his head. "What?"

The pirate looked off in the other direction, seeming agitated. The wiry-haired one shrugged. "Oh, right. I never introduced myself. I'm Bill or Wild Bill as most call me. And this here is my best friend Gus. We're working our way towards being special operatives. We're really good at it. Rescued a princess once too."

Alice laughed. "You were at the motel."

Bill nodded and then blushed. "Might have peeked in the window to check on you both and got an eye full." He looked Brad up and down slowly. "Did the government make you too? That how you got a willy that big? I've been asking for an enhancement. All I got was drugs. Lots of them, but they didn't make my dick bigger."

Brad wasn't sure how to respond. Even his wolf was stunned by the statement.

Alice broke into a fit of laughter.

Gus faced Alice's direction and lowered his head. Alice gasped and grabbed at Brad's shirt. "He knows Mae. She's not dead!"

"What? Wait, you can read him?"

"I can," said Alice. "But he's not like others either. Less noise in his head. Can't say the same for Bill. His head is pretty much chaos."

Bill smiled wide. "Oh yeah, we know Mae. We just met her. She believed us when Gus told her you were alive."

Brad held tighter to Alice. "She's okay? She made it out of the explosion?"

"Got herself mated to the one with the pink tips on the ends of his hair, but other than that, she's good. I mean, if you like your men British and all. I don't. Corbin is good to her. He and his friends are looking for you two, but they're looking in the wrong places. Gus here knows things, don't ya, Gus? He knew to go to the motel. Knew you'd need our help here tonight too. I told the others we'd get to save Red Riding Hood and the Big Bad Wolf. They never believe me though."

Alice pulled free from Brad and went towards the men. She stepped over a downed guard and walked right up to Gus, pulling him into a hug. She then did the same for Bill, making the man turn a few shades of pink in the process.

Alice looked to Brad, unshed tears of joy in her eyes. "She's okay."

Bill tugged at his lower lip. "James, the doctor back were we came from, says she's probably related to Brad. Something about an Asia Project or something. I don't know. But they think you were all tested on as babies. Think you got good drugs then too?"

Brad stiffened, thinking back to how overprotective he'd been of Mae and how his feelings for her had been on the opposite spectrum of sexual. Hearing the suggestion that she was somehow related to him fit. It felt right.

Alice beamed. "Can we go home now, please?"

He nodded. "I think so."

Bill threw his hands in the air. "I'll drive."

Gus stood perfectly still, his gaze meeting Brad's briefly. Bill groaned and then looked back at Brad. "Gus says hurry up. The place the guard with no hand or head came from has a tracking device implanted in you. It's tiny and they couldn't get a read when you were being held at the other place, but they can now that you're in the open. Gus says James can take it out without a problem." Bill opened the front of his leather jacket and pulled out a small baggie. "I got some of the good shit here if you want it for the pain. Helps me every time. But, uh, don't let the others there know. They take my stuff away all the time. They're big meanie heads."

They'd planted a tracking device on him? His gaze snapped to Alice. He'd put her in harm's way. He'd get her killed if he didn't put distance between them.

Running solves nothing.

Brad froze, the voice in his head new, one he'd never heard before. With a clear understanding of who had spoken to him mentally, he looked to the man dressed as a pirate.

Come with us now and our friends can see to your safety and the safe removal of the device. Run and you will forever run.

"They'll hurt her if they find me," said Brad, ignoring the questioning look Alice gave him.

Gus never moved as he spoke in Brad's head again. *If you come with us, she'll be safe and so will you. Run and she'll follow.*

Brad took a deep breath and then walked in the direction of Bill. He put his hand out. "Fine, but I'm driving. I saw your entrance and I'm pretty sure you're on drugs as we speak."

Bill tipped his head. "Are you saying you aren't?"

"Get in the van," barked Brad, liking the two men despite the fact they were both clearly crazy. He snorted. His rescue team looked like they could join the Village People at a moment's notice.

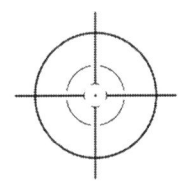

Chapter Fifteen

Alice sat, watching her husband talk with the group of men who had swarmed them within minutes of arriving. They'd barely gotten in the door before it seemed like they were sandwiched in the center of a group of muscular men, all of whom fired off question after question. Alice had yet to get all their names straight—though she was trying. She'd taken to thinking of them in terms such as, the Goth, the Scot, the Blond, the Grump and the Doctor.

Two of the men gave Bill and Gus quite a scolding about running off on their own. Bill maintained they'd had it all under control and that they should be made full-fledged special operatives as they had saved "Red Riding Hood and the Big Bad Wolf".

It was hard to see Bill and Gus as anything other than adorable. Though, Brad would have said otherwise after having to deal with the two men on the ride to PSI Headquarters. Alice hid her laugh as she thought back to Brad having to pull off to the side of the road to allow Bill to pee. It had taken some convincing, chasing, tackling and then flat out throwing the small man over Brad's shoulder to get Bill back in the vehicle. Gus had sat quietly in the van with Alice, his attention on something else entirely.

It was easy to see Bill and Gus were important to the PSI operatives. Even the grumpy one seemed worried about their well-being. If she was right, the Grump's name was Duke. After appearing relieved to see the two men alive and then questioning why they were dressed as a pimp and a pirate, Duke had yelled at them for daring to go off on their own in the first place.

Bill had yelled right back, accusing Duke of being a "big fat meanie-head".

Everyone at PSI seemed to really care for one another. They'd welcomed Brad and Alice with open arms and, it seemed, open hearts. The Doctor, or James if she had his name correct, had insisted he be allowed to check her and Brad over to make sure they were medically okay. Brad had been difficult to deal with during her exam, more than likely because alpha males tended to have issues with other men around their women. Plus, they liked to worry about everything to do with their mates. Thankfully, he finally calmed enough to speak with the others and answer their questions.

And they had a lot.

The Scot, a redhead with a long, thick beard who was wearing a kilt, kept making suggestive comments to her. They didn't bother Alice in the least. But they bothered her husband greatly. Brad had already punched the man twice, but the Scot kept going.

"Och, you like what you see?" he asked, his Scottish brogue strong as he caught her glancing in his direction. "I have that effect on the ladies."

"Striker," said the Goth, a man with long black hair with blue streaks in it. If she remembered right his name was Boomer or something close to it. "Her mate is going to beat the crap out of you if you keep pushing. You'll end up with the *Asshole of the Week* award—again."

Asshole of the Week Award?

She wanted to question what all that entailed, but she held back, enjoying the interplay too much to interrupt.

"Redheads make it all worth it," said Striker, waggling his brows at her, making her laugh. His gaze whipped to Boomer. "Visited the zoo lately?"

"Eat me," replied Boomer, lifting his

middle finger in the air.

"Och, yer nae my type, kitty."

The door to the room opened and Alice's heart hammered in her ears as she spotted Mae there, being led in by a tall, toned, blond man. A man she'd seen briefly on campus the night she'd been taken. No introductions were necessary. Alice knew the man to be Corbin at once. The very man Mae had been scheduled to go on a blind date with before they'd both been captured.

She was up and out of the chair in record time, racing past Brad and at Mae. Squealing, Mae threw her arms out and the two collided, spinning in a circle, laughing and crying as they held one another. It took a bit for Alice to realize the room had fallen silent. She paused, still holding her best friend.

"Why are they all staring at us?" she asked.

Mae snorted. "Because they don't know what to do when one woman cries, let alone two. For smart, powerful males, they're pretty much rendered useless if a woman and tears are involved."

Alice smiled. "They're all adorable."

Duke grunted and tugged at his black T-shirt that read *Team Edward* of all things. "I'm not fucking adorable."

Mae laughed. "Oh, Duke, you totally are."

He groaned and then glanced at the floor, mumbling something about women and how they shouldn't be allowed in headquarters. No one paid him any mind.

Brad moved forward and extended his hand to Corbin. "Glad to see you made it out alive. Thank you for protecting Mae."

"No," said Corbin, a British accent evident. "Thank you for what you did for my mate. You were there for her until I could reach her. Has James informed you of our findings?"

Brad nodded and then smiled down at Mae. "Looks like we're family."

The way he said it made Alice's heart swell

even more for the man. Her best friend and her husband were related and that tickled her beyond belief.

Mae beamed and tossed her arms around Brad, hugging him tight. She cried more, patting Brad as she righted herself. She glanced between Brad and Alice, wiped her cheeks and then spoke, "The two of you are mated?"

Alice nodded and Brad took her hand in his, bringing it to his lips and kissing it gently. "Yes. I did the unthinkable. I tied myself to *one* man for the rest of my life."

Brad chuckled, taking her comment in good nature. "Don't sound too thrilled."

She wanted to run her hands all over his sexy body and have her way with him right then and there. She held back, although her inner harlot was on board with the idea as well. "You're just lucky that I love you."

Bending, he kissed her lips quickly. "Nah, that was a given. I told you I'm a ladies' man. I'd have been more shocked if you didn't fall for me instantly."

"Oh please." She rolled her eyes, making Mae laugh.

Brad took a deep breath and then put his forehead against Alice's. "I love you too, baby."

Mae squealed again and clapped. "Wait. You do know she's totally hyper, has a wicked temper and is stubborn, right?"

"Redheads are totally worth it," added Striker from the sidelines, making everyone laugh.

"So I'm learning," replied Brad.

Corbin cleared his throat and the mood in the room grew somber. "Brad, my men filled me in over the phone on what you told them about your past dealings with PSI. They tell me you were recruited by Vepkhia."

Alice watched as Brad's posture went rigid. "Yes," he said, his jaw tight. "So was my best friend Vic."

Corbin glanced around the room and then

cleared his throat. "We've had an issue with rogues that only came to light recently. I reached out to other teams within PSI and other divisions around the world, but Vepkhia hasn't been heard from in nearly a year. It looks as though he went missing around the same time you and your friend did."

"Did he sell Vic and me out?" demanded Brad.

Alice rubbed his arm, hoping to keep his wolf calm. She didn't really want to see what would happen if he lost control in a room full of shifter males. There was so much alpha energy in the room as it was that she doubted it would end well.

Corbin shook his head. "Honestly, we don't know. There was a time I'd have said no, but I can't say that with any certainty now. What I can tell you is that his division of PSI got back to me and informed me that they have paperwork on file for both you and your friend. It appears that Vepkhia was legitimately bringing you on as Shadow Agents. We don't know what happened after that or where he is. If he didn't betray PSI and you, that would mean…"

"The Corporation killed him," said Brad evenly.

"Correct."

"I'm worried they killed Vic too."

Corbin nodded. "As are we. We're also concerned for two of our agents who were undercover at the facility."

Alice gasped. "Ezra?"

"Yes, as well as Caesar. Both are good men and great agents. We haven't been able to establish contact with either."

A tall man with black, shoulder-length hair entered. He grinned and held out papers to Corbin. "Captain, General Newman sent these over."

"Thank you, Malik." Corbin took the papers and grinned before handing them to

Brad. "It would appear that you were not only approved nearly a year ago to be a Shadow Agent, but you've been on the payroll all this time as well. Here is a list of the funds to date. There are details here on temporary housing offered to all operatives and everything else you need to know."

Alice stiffened. "Wait. What does this all mean?"

Mae took her hand. "Alice, it means your husband and my husband work together. It also means you and Brad are starting a new life together."

Alice smiled and then looked to her husband. "I'm finishing my schooling and getting my degree. I already know you're going to worry about me. But James checked me and I don't have bad guy lowjacking on me. And yours has been removed. I'm going back to classes."

Corbin grunted.

Mae flashed a wide smile. "I'm having the

same argument with mine too. Our men are very headstrong and protective."

"They can suck it," said Alice, crossing her arms under her breasts. "I worked really hard for that degree and I'm close to getting it. No bad guys are stopping me from my education."

Striker lifted his hand. "I'd be happy to babysit them on campus."

Duke stood. "You just want to go back to the campus because you got all those numbers from the hot little co-eds. You're not fooling anyone, Striker."

"Hey, two birds…" offered Striker. "Or one cock, lots of co-eds."

Brad glanced over the paperwork before him and then faced Alice. "I promise you that we'll make sure both of you can finish your schooling, but you need to let us all make sure you're each safe first."

Alice winked. "Of course, stud muffin."

He groaned.

Mae laughed.

THE END

Dear Reader

Did you enjoy this title and want to know more about Mandy M. Roth, her pen names and all the titles she has available for purchase (over 100)?

About Mandy:

New York Times & *USA TODAY* Bestselling Author Mandy M. Roth is a self-proclaimed Goonie, loves 80s music and movies and wishes leg warmers would come back into fashion. She also thinks the movie *The Breakfast Club* should be mandatory viewing for...okay, everyone. When she's not dancing around her office to the sounds of the 80s or writing books, she can be found designing book covers for New York publishers, small presses, and indie authors.

Learn More:

To learn more about Mandy and her pen names, please visit http://

www.mandyroth.com

For latest news about Mandy's newest releases and sales subscribe to her newsletter

http://www.mandyroth.com/newsletter/

To join Mandy's Facebook Reader Group: The Roth Heads, please visit

https://www.facebook.com/groups/MandyRothReaders/

Review this title:

Please let others know if you enjoyed this title. Consider leaving an honest review on the vendor site in which you purchased this title. Reviews help to spread the word and boost overall sales. This means more books in the series you love.

Thank you!

Mandy has included a FREE excerpt from her book Gabe's Fortune (Prospect Springs Shifters for your enjoyment.

Wolf's Surrender: Part of the Immortal Ops World

Copyright © 2016

New Frontier Territory, Prospect Springs, just outside the town of Cutter Grove

Gabriel MacSweeny surveyed his newest acquisition to the best of his ability considering it spanned a large area. It was cathartic to look out and over it all, even though dust was kicking up and threatening to burn his eyes. He'd been in worse weather. Hell, back in his days in the World Guard, he'd once had to hunker down for six days to ride out a dust storm that had claimed The Plains for nearly a week—paralyzing everything in its path. The state of things today was more a nuisance than anything. Though, he'd seen a few people walking around with bandanas over their mouths and noses.

Lightweights.

The dust made it slightly harder to appreciate his purchase. The sheer size of the purchase was more of an issue. Unless he found higher ground, he'd never see all of it at once. That pleased him greatly. Where there had been nothing more than hard, cracked earth and no vegetation as far as the eye was able to see, now rested train cars, wagons, horses and steel steeds. A band of misfits pulled together by circumstance.

His kind of people.

He wasn't exactly normal, and while most of the people in his hometown knew as much, he didn't advertise the news in his extensive travels. It wasn't easy to predict what type of reception a supernatural would get within different boundaries of the New Frontier Territories. Some were welcoming of supernaturals. Others would just as soon see him dragged behind a horse than have him there among their women and children.

As if Gabriel would ever harm a woman or a child. He wasn't that type of man. None of his family was, yet they all still hid in plain sight. They all tried their best to minimize the number of people who knew without a shadow of a doubt what they were.

Shapeshifters.

Men who had the ability to turn into animals. In the case of the MacSweenys, their family animal was a wolf—at least for the most part. Some were different animals, but most were wolves. And there was the addition of magik in some of the MacSweenys, such as Gabriel and his brothers.

From all Gabriel had been told of the world before the Great Sickness, supernaturals had never been welcome anywhere. Most people hadn't even believed they were real back then.

Fools.

The old books, now locked away for preservation, spoke of a period before the Great Sickness, a time when the world was overpopulated. A time when mankind spent more time at war with each other than worrying about the planet and the damage they were doing to it. The result of their carelessness had been the Great Sickness—a product of pollution, technology and germ warfare—that had happened nearly seven hundred years ago.

Though no one was certain that was what had caused it all. Fear of a repeat of the mass deaths had some territories banning technologies. The penalties in those territories or areas were swift and severe. Often even death. Other areas openly welcomed technology and advancements. Gabriel felt a balance between the two was the best course of action, as his home boundary and town of Prospect Springs believed as well.

Pride welled as he looked over his purchase. This would be a way to hide in plain sight while still traveling—something he loved to do. Growing up in Prospect Springs, part of the New Frontier Territory, had been good. He couldn't complain, but it had done little to satisfy the explorer in him. The young boy who had wanted to travel the world, meet others and experience everything he could.

He spun his cane around, still in a jovial

mood. The silver from the wolf's head on the top of his cane burned his skin, but he didn't mind. He liked the bite of pain. It was a constant reminder of what he was. The cane wasn't required for any purpose, other than in it was a sword he liked to keep on hand. One never knew what one would run into while traveling, and turning into a wolf wasn't always the best option in a fight.

Sometimes, you had to distinguish when to fight like a man or a beast.

Gabriel ran his hand over his upper lip, considering re-growing the rather obnoxious mustache and goatee he'd only recently shaved. His brothers had ribbed him endlessly about his facial hair. They weren't exactly clean-shaven, but they'd never had a goatee the length he'd allowed his to be.

Homesickness swept over him. Perched on the edge of Cutter's Grove—a few day's ride to Prospect Springs—Gabriel smiled, knowing he'd see his family soon enough. It had been far too long between visits home. He hadn't told any of them about his new acquisition. They'd be shocked when they saw what he bought.

Gabriel soaked in the sights of his carnival. It amused him greatly. It was something more along the lines of a traveling circus. He could still remember attending carnivals when he was a young boy. His aunts and his mother would take all the boys to the edges of town, and for one magical night, their lives had been transformed. The MacSweenys had no longer been the oddities in the town. Freaks had poured in and relished the attention, drawing the focus to the carnival and from the MacSweeny boys.

Giving them all some welcome relief.

Not to mention the carnival's arrival had meant Gabriel would be whisked away into a different type of world—one that felt like a living storybook, an adventure under canvas tents. It still held the same wonder for him now as it had when he was but a child. Though now he chose to be part of it.

To belong to something offbeat.

He wasn't friendly with any of the carny folk yet. He'd only been introduced to a select few by the previous owner. The man who had sold him the entire carnival, including all the existing contracts with the workers and their pay notes, had been well beyond the point of retirement age. He, unlike Gabriel, was not immortal. Life had been hard and taken its toll upon the man. He'd smelled heavily of sickness, and Gabriel knew without being told why the man had been desperate to find his carnival a good owner.

Death was upon the man's doorstep, and Gabriel knew the Reaper would arrive before the month's end and claim its due. From what the man had confessed, the carnival had run into issues a few territories back, leaving three of their own dead at the hands of humanists — those who didn't tolerate anything beyond pure humans and didn't take kindly to supernaturals near them and theirs. The previous owner had tried hard to protect those who worked for him—his family, he'd called them—but his efforts had fallen short. When he'd learned Gabriel's secret, he'd looked so relieved, offering him the carnival then and there, at a rate any smart man would have been stupid to refuse.

And Gabriel, while many things, was not a stupid man.

Gabriel had a stand-up reputation as a businessman, and while he'd never ventured into the business of carnivals or circuses before, he knew how to turn a profit in his endeavors. The old man had parted with the carnival for less than he should have. It wasn't for lack of Gabriel trying to pay him a fair price. He'd simply refused to take all of what was offered to him. He'd gone on and on about how Gabriel would do right by his family, his people, and that he could die in peace knowing so.

As Gabriel looked around, he questioned if they'd be open and receptive to him—someone they believed to be human. For now, he'd let them think as much. It was easier that way. They'd be less on guard with him that way, even with the ugly events in their recent past. He, like the previous owner, had a strong sense that someone within the carnival had been part of the trouble—part of the reason three had died and nearly ten more had been hurt. Gabriel would ferret out the culprit, or culprits if that was the case, out and see to it they answered for their crimes.

He only hoped his suspicions were wrong. It was hard to believe any here would turn on the other, but the smell of humans among the carny folk rode the air. He didn't automatically distrust humans, but he'd learned long ago they were as deadly, if not more so, than others like him. Plus, he knew some of the element that was attracted to the traveling lifestyle had sordid pasts—some were even criminals or con-artists.

He'd weed those out and judge them for himself. He'd honor the owner's last wishes of keeping the carny family safe even if it was from themselves. He was a man of his word after all. Often, a man only had his word to hang his hat on.

Already, tents were popping up everywhere, dotting the horizon as the sights and sounds of people buzzed through the air. Pride continued to swell in him. He'd acted rashly, buying the carnival without putting too much thought behind it. But it had felt right.

His gut had demanded he act upon the urge to purchase. That he own it at all costs. He knew better than to ignore a deep calling. The carnival turned a profit even in parts of the New Frontier Territory where people didn't have much coin to spread around. Gabriel considered avoiding those areas so the good people there wouldn't be tempted to spend little they had, but he knew how much they looked forward to the carnival rolling in to town. He'd not take that from them.

Besides, his carnival was the best-priced one out there. The sad truth was a good deal of the New Frontier Territory didn't have a pot to piss in. Yet, for the most part, the people were happy. Pockets of money existed, and more and more, Gabriel could see things starting to change for the better. In no way were they as well off as the Old Territory. It was hard to have everyone up to that level of living.

He took comfort in the knowledge his newest purchase managed to bring happiness and joy to people in desperate situations. It meant something to him. He'd figure out a way to continue to turn a profit, keep the workers safe and happy while making sure those in impoverished areas were still offered the experience of the show.

The magik of it all.

Tumbleweed blew past. He silently cursed for what he'd gotten himself into. The southeast section of New Frontier Territory hadn't seen water in months and was hotter than a stick of dynamite lit on both ends. If something didn't give soon, he'd likely burst into flames before he had his first official opening night. He had big plans for the carnival. For now he needed to focus on getting rid of any acts that ripped off patrons. A clean-running operation was what he was looking for. There were plenty of acts who were what they claimed. He didn't need anyone making their dime by stealing from those less fortunate.

A large bald man approached, his handlebar mustache looking well-maintained and out of place with the current trends in men's facial hair. The tight pants he wore were comical, but Gabriel kept his laughter to himself. The man had to be Gusto. The strong man he'd heard so much about. Gabriel didn't want to point out he could lift more than the human male, so he offered a gentle smile. If Gusto needed to feel like the biggest, baddest guy around, Gabriel would permit it.

At least for now.

END EXCERPT

Gabe's Fortune (Prospect Springs Shifters) is

available for purchase from all major e-book vendors. Details can be found on Mandy's website www.mandyroth.com

Mandy M. Roth, Online

Mandy loves hearing from readers and can be found interacting on social media.
(copy & paste links into your browser window)

Website: http://www.MandyRoth.com

Blog:
http://www.MandyRoth.com/blog
Facebook: http://www.facebook.com/AuthorMandyRoth

Twitter: @MandyMRoth

Book Release Newsletter: mandyroth.com/newsletter.htm
(Newsletters: I do not share emails and only send newsletters when there is a new release/contest/or sales)

Printed in Great Britain
by Amazon